John Churton Collins

From Shakespeare to Pope

An inquiry into the causes and phenomena of the rise of classical poetry in

England

John Churton Collins

From Shakespeare to Pope
An inquiry into the causes and phenomena of the rise of classical poetry in England

ISBN/EAN: 9783337104146

Printed in Europe, USA, Canada, Australia, Japan

Cover: Foto ©Andreas Hilbeck / pixelio.de

More available books at **www.hansebooks.com**

THE

QUARTERLY REVIEW.

VOL. 163.

PUBLISHED IN

JULY & OCTOBER, 1886.

LONDON:

JOHN MURRAY, ALBEMARLE STREET.

1886

CONTENTS

OF

No. 326.

THE
QUARTERLY REVIEW.

ᴎ Aʀᴛ. I.—*From Shakespeare to Pope. An Inquiry into the Causes and Phenomena of the Rise of Classical Poetry in England.* By Edmund Gosse, Clark Lecturer on English Literature at the University of Cambridge. Cambridge: at the University Press. 1885.

THAT such a book as this should have been permitted to go forth to the world with the *imprimatur* of the University of Cambridge, affords matter for very grave reflection. But it is a confirmation of what we have long suspected. It is one more proof that those rapid and reckless innovations, which have during the last few years completely changed the faces of our Universities, have not been made with impunity. We are no sticklers for the old regime, no advocates of a policy of ultra-Conservatism. We think that the Universities have done wisely in extending the ancient boundaries of education, and that those boundaries might with advantage be extended still further. We should, for example, be heartily glad to hear that Oxford and Cambridge had provided as amply for the interpretation of Modern Literature as they have for the interpretation of Ancient : that the Laocoon was being studied side by side with the Poetics, and Macbeth side by side with the Agamemnon. But there are certain points on which the Universities cannot be too Conservative. There are certain points on which any departure from prescription and tradition is not merely to be regretted, but to be deprecated. Whatever concessions Oxford and Cambridge may find it desirable to make in consulting the interests of modern life, it should be their first care to guard jealously their own prerogatives. Of all revolutions, that would be the most disastrous to learning and culture which should subject University legislation to popular control. Six centuries have not altered the relative position in which Oxford and Cambridge stand to the outside world. In the infancy of civilization they preserved learning from extinction. As civilization advances, they have the more difficult task of preserving it from corruption. They have no longer to combat barbarism and dulness, sloth and ignorance, but to counteract the mischievous activity of agencies scarcely less antagonistic to all that it is their glory to uphold.

It may sound paradoxical to say that the more widely education spreads, the more generally intelligent a nation becomes, the greater is the danger to which Art and Letters are exposed. And yet how obviously is this the case, and how easily is this explained. The quality of skilled work depends mainly on the standard required of the workman. If his judges and patrons belong to the discerning few who, knowing what is excellent, are intolerant of everything which falls short of excellence, the standard required will necessarily be a high one, and the standard required will be the standard attained. In past times, for example, the only men of letters who were respected formed a portion of that highly cultivated class who will always be in the minority; and to that class, and to that class only, they appealed. A community within a community, they regarded the general public with as much indifference as the general public regarded them, and wrote only for themselves, and for those who stood on the same intellectual level as themselves. It was so in the Athens of Pericles; it was so in the Rome of Augustus; it was so in the Florence of the Medici; and a striking example of the same thing is to be found in our own Elizabethan Dramatists. Though their bread depended on the brutal and illiterate savages for whose amusement they catered, they still talked the language of scholars and poets, and forced their rude hearers to sit out works which could have been intelligible only to scholars and poets. Each felt with pride that he belonged to a great guild, which neither had nor affected to have anything in common with the multitude. Each strove only for the applause of those whose praise is not lightly given. Each spurred the other on. When Marlowe worked, he worked with the fear of Greene before his eyes, as Shakspeare was put on his mettle by Jonson, and Jonson by Shakspeare. We owe Much Ado about Nothing and the Alchemist not to men who bid only for the suffrage of the mob, but to men who stood in awe of the verdict which would be passed on them by the company assembled at the Mermaid and the Devil.

As long as men of letters continue to form an intellectual aristocracy, and, stimulated by mutual rivalry, strain every nerve to excel, and as long also—and this is a condition equally important—

important—as they have no temptation to pander to the crowd, so long will Literature maintain its dignity, and so long will the standard attained in Literature be a high one. In the days of Dryden and Pope, in the days even of Johnson and Gibbon, the greater part of the general public either read nothing, or read nothing but politics and sermons. The few who were interested in Poetry, in Criticism, in History, were, as a rule, those who had received a learned education, men of highly cultivated tastes and of considerable attainments. A writer, therefore, who aspired to contribute to polite literature, had to choose between finding no readers at all, and finding such readers as he was bound to respect—between instant oblivion, and satisfying a class which, composed of scholars, would have turned with contempt from writings unworthy of scholars. A classical style, a refined tone, and an adequate acquaintance with the chief authors of Ancient Rome and of Modern France, were requisites, without which even a periodical essayist would have had small hope of obtaining a hearing. Whoever will turn, we do not say to the papers of Addison and his circle in the early part of the last century, or to those of Chesterfield and his circle later on, but to the average critical work of Cave's and Dodsley's hack writers, cannot fail to be struck with its remarkable merit in point of literary execution.

But as education spreads, a very different class of readers call into being a very different class of writers. Men and women begin to seek in books the amusement or excitement which they sought formerly in social dissipation. To the old public of scholars succeeds a public, in which every section of society has its representatives, and to provide this vast body with the sort of reading which is acceptable to it, becomes a thriving and lucrative calling. An immense literature springs up, which has no other object than to catch the popular ear, and no higher aim than to please for the moment. That perpetual craving for novelty, which has in all ages been characteristic of the multitude, necessitates in authors of this class a corresponding rapidity of production. The writer of a single good book is soon forgotten by his contemporaries; but the writer of a series of bad books is sure of reputation and emolument. Indeed, a good book and a bad book stand, so far as the general public are concerned, on precisely the same level, as they meet with precisely the same fate. Each presents the attraction of a new title-page. Each is glanced through, and tossed aside. Each is estimated not by its intrinsic worth, but according to the skill with which it has been puffed. Till within comparatively recent times this literature was for the most part represented by

novels

novels and poems, and by those light and desultory essays, sketches and *ana*, which are the staple commodity of our magazines. And so long as it confined itself within these bounds it did no mischief, and even some good. Flimsy and superficial though it was, it had at least the merit of interesting thousands in Art and Letters, who would otherwise have been indifferent to them. It afforded nutriment to minds which would have rejected more solid fare. To men of business and pleasure who, though no longer students, still retained the tincture of early culture, it offered the most agreeable of all methods of killing time, while scholars found in it welcome relaxation from severer studies. It thus supplied a want. Presenting attractions not to one class only, but to all classes, it grew on the world. Its patrons, who half a century ago numbered thousands, now number millions. And as it has grown in favour, it has grown in ambition. It is no longer satisfied with the humble province which it once held, but is extending its dominion in all directions. It has its representatives in every department of Art and Letters. It has its poets, its critics, its philosophers, its historians. It crowds not our club tables and news-stalls only, but our libraries. And so what was originally a mere excrescence on literature in the proper sense of the term, has now assumed proportions so gigantic, that it has not merely overshadowed that literature, but threatens to supersede it.

No thoughtful man can contemplate the present condition of current literature without disgust and alarm. We have still, indeed, lingering among us a few masters whose works would have been an honour to any age ; and here and there among writers may be discerned men who are honourably distinguished by a conscientious desire to excel, men who respect themselves, and respect their calling. But to say that these are in the minority, would be to give a very imperfect idea of the proportion which their numbers bear to those who figure most prominently before the public. They are, in truth, as tens are to myriads. Their comparative insignificance is such, that they are powerless even to leaven the mass. The position which they would have occupied half a century ago, and which they may possibly occupy half a century hence, is now usurped by a herd of scribblers who have succeeded, partly by sheer force of numbers, and partly by judicious co-operation, in all but dominating literature. Scarcely a day passes in which some book is not hurried into the world, which owes its existence not to any desire on the part of its author to add to the stores of useful literature, or even to a hope of obtaining money, but simply to that paltry vanity which thrives on the sort of homage

of

of which society of a certain kind is not grudging, and which knows no distinction between notoriety and fame. A few years ago a man who contributed articles to a current periodical, or who delivered a course of lectures, had, as a rule, the good sense to know that when they had fulfilled the purpose for which they were originally intended, the world had no more concern with them, and he would as soon have thought of inflicting them in the shape of a volume, on the public, as he would have thought of issuing an edition of his private letters to his friends. Now all is changed. The first article in the creed of a person, who has figured in either of these capacities, appears to be that he is bound to force himself into notice in the character of an author. And this, happily for himself, but unhappily for the interests of literature, he is able to do with perfect facility and with perfect impunity. Books are speedily manufactured, and as speedily reduced to pulp. It is as easy to invest a worthless book with those superficial attractions which catch the eye of the crowd, as it is a meritorious one. As the general public are the willing dupes of puffers, it is no more difficult to palm off on them the spurious wares of literary charlatans, than it is to beguile them into purchasing the wares of any other sort of charlatan. No one is interested in telling them the truth. Many, on the contrary, are interested in deceiving them. As a rule, the men who write bad books are the men who criticize bad books; and as they know that what they mete out in their capacity of judges to-day is what will in turn be meted out to them in their capacity of authors to-morrow, it is not surprising that their relations should be similar to those which Tacitus tells us existed between Vinius and Tigellinus—'nulla innocentiæ cura, sed vices impunitatis.' The Edinburgh and Quarterly Reviews appear unfortunately to have abandoned, for the most part, to Reviews of a very different character the censorship of current publications.

Meanwhile all those vile arts which were formerly confined to the circulators of bad novels and bad poems are practised without shame. It is shocking, it is disgusting to contemplate the devices to which many men of letters will stoop for the sake of exalting themselves into a factitious reputation. And the evil is fast spreading. Indeed, things have come to such a pass, that persons of real merit, if they have the misfortune to depend on their pens for a livelihood, must either submit to be elbowed and jostled out of the field, or take part in the same ignoble scramble for notoriety, and the same detestable system of mutual puffery. Thus everything which formerly tended to raise the standard of literary ambition and literary attainment has given place

place to everything which tends to degrade it. The multitude now stand where the scholar once stood. From the multitude emanate, to the multitude are dedicated, two-thirds of the publications which pour forth each year in myriads from our presses—

> ' viviamo scorti
> Da mediocrità : sceso il sapiente
> E salita è la turba a un sol confine
> Che il mondo agguaglia.'

All this is no doubt inevitable, but what we sincerely trust is not inevitable is the corruption of that small minority, whose standards are not the standards of the crowd. The nurseries and strongholds of that minority are the Universities. At the Universities are still studied in a spirit too narrow indeed, but reverently and conscientiously, those masterpieces which, so long as they shall continue to be studied, will be of power to purify and exalt. There, amid the din of voices blatant without —the puffing and the cant, the gushing and the cackle—the still small voice of sincerity is clear. No shallow dilettantism has as yet found footing there. No sciolist, no pretender, no dishonest worker, has ever escaped detection and condemnation there. Nothing which falls short of a standard, as high perhaps as it could possibly be, is tolerated either in those who teach, or in those who seek honours in the schools. What work is done, is done as legislators, whose moral and intellectual ideals have been derived from Thucydides and Aristotle, from Plato and Sophocles, would necessarily insist upon its being done. And may this continue. For as long as this continues, as long as the Universities remain true to tradition and true to themselves, so long amid the general corruption will Art and Learning be sound at the core.

But we have lately observed symptoms which are, we fear, no uncertain indications that even the Universities have not escaped contagion. It is not our intention here to offer any remarks on the extraordinary innovations which have recently been made in the old system, both at Oxford and Cambridge. That the majority of them are mere reckless experiments, that some of them are positively pernicious, and that almost all of them are fraught with peril, is, we think, unquestionable. If any proof of what these innovations are likely to lead to were needed, it would be afforded by the volume which stands at the head of this article. We have already pointed out the enormous responsibility which rests with the Universities at the present time. We have shown what was indeed self-
evident,

evident, that unless they continue to oppose the true faith to the false faith, the high standard to the low standard, the excellent to the mediocre, the sound to the unsound, the prospects of literature are mournful indeed. It is therefore with the greatest regret that we have had placed in our hands, dated from Trinity College, Cambridge, and published by the University Press, a work which we do not scruple to describe as most derogatory to all concerned in its production. Whether this volume is an indication of the manner in which the important subject with which it deals is studied at Cambridge, we do not know. We sincerely trust that it is not. But of two things we are very sure; first, that a book so unworthy, in everything but externals, of a great University has never before been given to the world; and secondly, that it is the bounden duty of all friends of learning to join in discountenancing so evil a precedent.

Not the least mischievous characteristic of the work is the skill with which its worthlessness is disguised. From title to colophon there is, so far as externals are concerned, everything to disarm suspicion, everything to inspire trust. An excellent index; unexceptionable type; unexceptionable paper;

'Chartæ regiæ, novi libri,
Novi umbilici, lora rubra, membrana
Directa plumbo, et pumice omnia æquata.'

On opening the volume our confidence redoubles. We turn to the Preface. We there learn that the substance of the work was delivered in the form of lectures to members of the University of Cambridge in the Hall of Trinity College.

'It has been,' says Mr. Gosse, 'no small advantage to me that among the distinguished listeners to whom I have had the honour of reading these pages, there have been more than a few whose special studies have rendered them particularly acute in criticising. In consequence of such criticism I have been able profitably to revise the work, to add evidence where it seemed wanting, to remove rash statements, and to remould ambiguous sentences.'

In the course of the work we learn that many 'eminent friends' have been anxiously consulted; for 'in an enquiry of this nature,' observes the author, 'exact evidence, even of a minute kind, outweighs in importance any expression of mere critical opinion.' As we are not concerned with Mr. Gosse's eminent friends, but only with Mr. Gosse himself, we shall merely remark that we quite absolve Professor Gardiner and Mr. Austin Dobson from all complicity in Mr. Gosse's delinquencies.

Of all offences of which a writer can be guilty, the most detestable

detestable is that of simulating familiarity with works which he knows only at second hand, or of which he knows nothing more than the title. That a Lecturer on English Literature should not know whether the Arcadia of Sidney, and the Oceana of Harrington, are in prose or verse, or, not knowing, should not have taken the trouble to ascertain, is discreditable enough ; but that he should, under the impression that they are poems, have had the effrontery to sit in judgment on them, might well, in Macaulay's favourite phrase, make us ashamed of our species. And yet this is what Mr. Gosse has done. In one place (page 26), he classes and compares the Arcadia with the Faery Queen. In another place (page 75), he classes and compares it with Giles Fletcher's Christ's Victory and Triumph ; while on page 26 the Oceana, coupled with the Arcadia, is compared, on the one hand with Spenser's poem, and on the other hand with Phineas Fletcher's Purple Island.* Of the gross chronological blunder of which he is guilty, in placing the Oceana with the Arcadia, and the Faery Queen in the 'great generation,' when the Oceana was published in 1656, a period long subsequent to the time of which he is speaking, we say nothing. It is easy to see what has misled him with regard to the ' Oceana,' and his error certainly furnishes a very amusing illustration of his method of investigation. He has confounded James Harrington, the prose writer, who was born in 1611, with Sir John Harrington, the poet, who was born in 1561 ; and the title ' Oceana ' having a very poetical sound, he has jumped to the conclusion that it is a poem.

On page 108, he informs us that Garth's Claremont is ' a

---

* As this may seem incredible to those of our readers who do not know what modern bookmakers are capable of, we will give the passages with their contexts in full. ' Poetry began to be written for poets, for the elect, for a circle ; and this was one of the deadly effects of that curious embargo upon publication, of which I have spoken. Utter disregard was paid to unity, to proportion, to extent. In the great generation there had been too little regard for these qualities. Without profanity be it spoken, Sidney's " Arcadia " is dreadfully amorphous and invertebrate, and Macaulay's difficulty of being in at the death of the "Blatant Beast" would never have been propounded, if the " Faery Queen " had not been so long, that it is really excusable not to be aware that the "Blatant Beast" does not die. But if the "Arcadia" is shapeless, what are we to say of " Oceana "? and let him not call the " Faery Queen " tedious or dull who has never grappled with Phineas Fletcher's " Purple Island."' (Pp. 25, 26.) ' The heroic poems of the Elizabethan and Jacobean ages,—" The Barons' Wars " of Drayton, the "Albion's England " of Warner, the " Ovid's Banquet of Sense " of Chapman, for instance, had possessed various brilliant and touching qualities, irregular force and sudden brilliance of style, but certainly not what Hobbes meant by " perspicuity and facility of construction." The " Arcadia " of Sidney is not facile, the " Christ's Victory and Triumph " of Giles Fletcher is not in this sense perspicuous ; but Waller's " Battle of the Summer Islands " is, just as " The Hind and the Panther " of Dryden is perspicuous, and " The Dunciad " admirable for its facility of construction. (Page 75.)

direct

direct imitation of Denham's Cooper's Hill.' If he had taken the trouble to read Garth's poem, he would have seen that, beyond the fact that it derives its title from the name of a place, and that it is written in heroics, it has simply nothing in common with Cooper's Hill. Denham's poem is, as we need scarcely say, a poem describing the prospect from Cooper's Hill — St. Paul's, Windsor, the Thames, the valley of the Thames—and with that description are interwoven such reflections as these objects severally call up; it then goes on to describe, and to describe with singular animation, a stag-hunt ; and it concludes with some remarks bearing immediately on contemporary politics, suggested by the view of Runnymede. Garth's poem, on the other hand, is simply a *jeu d'esprit* written on the occasion of the name of Claremont being given to the villa founded at Esher by the Earl of Clare. As a stream took its rise in the hill on which the mansion stood, welling up in a grotto where there was an echo, it struck Garth that he might make out of this a pretty story in the manner of Ovid. And so, with a few general remarks on the venality of poets who are ready to flatter without distinction any one who will pay them, and with the assurance that his own desire to please his noble patron springs from the most disinterested motives, he goes on to say that he has no intention of describing Claremont and its beauties. That theme he leaves to a nobler muse; his task is merely to tell

'how ancient fame
Records from whence the villa took its name,'

and the legend of Montano and Echo, modelled on the legend of Narcissus and Echo, in the third book of the Metamorphoses begins. With that legend we do not propose to trouble our readers. It is as easy to see what has misled Mr. Gosse in this case, as in the other case. Indeed, Garth himself has set the trap, and a reader who went no further than the title and the first words of the preface, would be certain to be caught. ' They who have seen,' he writes, 'those two excellent poems of Cooper's Hill and Windsor Forest, will show a great deal of candour if they approve of this.' What Garth meant of course was, as his work sufficiently proves, not to institute any comparison between his poems and the poems of Denham and Pope, but to obviate the objections of those who might perhaps expect to find in a poem taking its title from a place, what they had found in other poems taking their titles from places.

But these are not the only examples of Mr. Gosse's offences on this score. On page 102 he describes Daniel's Cleopatra,

and

and Philotas as ' choral tragi-comedies.' If he had consulted
them, he would have .seen that they are pure tragedies in the
most monotonously stilted style of pure classical tragedy. Again
on page 102 we are told that Denham's Sophy 'remains a
solitary specimen of the Seneca tragedy amongst the English
dramas of the age, just as the curious play of Tyr et Sidon
remains a solitary experiment in romantic tragedy in 17th-
century French.' Will our readers credit that the play thus
confidently asserted to be a ' specimen of Seneca tragedy' has
absolutely no point in common with Seneca's plays? It is a
drama as purely romantic as Lear or Hamlet. It does not
observe the unities, except perhaps the unity of place ; it has
no Chorus ; one of the characters is obviously modelled on
the Shakspearian Clown ; * part of it is written in rhyme, part
of it in prose, and part of it in blank verse so loose and
straggling as to be scarcely distinguishable from prose. But
to proceed. Mr. Gosse speaks on page 118 of Fanshawe's
'little epic of Dido and Æneas;' Fanshawe's little epic, as
he would have seen if he had turned to it, is neither more
nor less than a translation of Virgil's Fourth Æneid in the
Spenserian stanza. On page 25, Henry More's philosophical
allegory, the Psychozoia, is described as an epic poem! On
page 247 he informs us that the Faery Queen was re-written
by an anonymous hand in 1687. What this anonymous hand
re-wrote was simply the first book ; and as the volume was
licensed in 1686, we presume that it was written not in 1687,
but in or before 1686. On the same page we are told that
Butler, the author of Hudibras, ' re-wrote some of his most
characteristic pieces which had been composed in the older
prosody to conform them to the taste he had acquired.' He re-
wrote exactly one poem, the Elephant in the Moon.

There are many things in Mr. Gosse's volume, as we shall
presently show, which prove his utter incapacity for the task he
has undertaken, but nothing is more derogatory to him than his
habitual inaccuracy with respect to dates. However limited a
man's reading may be, however treacherous his memory, however slender his abilities, he has no excuse for making blunders
of this kind. It is plain that Mr. Gosse, so far from attempting
to verify his dates, has not even troubled himself to consult the
title-pages of the works to which he refers. We will give a few
examples. He says on page 165, speaking of the heroic
quatrain, that Hobbes ' adopted it for his translation of Homer,

---

* The character of Solyman. See the dialogue between him and the King,
act i. scene 2 : and, again, the dialogue between him and the Tormentors, act iv.
scene 1.

and this was followed a dozen years later by Dryden's Annus. Mirabilis.' Now the first instalment of Hobbes's Homer was his translation of four books of the Odyssey published in 1674, then followed his version of the whole Iliad in 1675, and of the whole Odyssey in 1677. Dryden's Annus Mirabilis was published in 1667, seven years before the first instalment of Hobbes's Homer. Mr. Gosse tells us (p. 234) that Oldham died in 1684. Oldham died in December 1683. He informs us (p. 64) that certain verses quoted from Fenton were 'sung' by that poet in 1730. The verses occur in the dedication of Fenton's well-known edition of Waller's Poems, which was published in 1729. He informs us (p. 252) that in 1684 Roscommon 'threw off the constraint of rhyme in his Art of Poetry.' Roscommon's Art of Poetry, or rather his translation of Horace's. Ars Poetica, the work to which Mr. Gosse with characteristic slovenliness alludes, appeared in 1680. Speaking of the year 1642, he says: 'Ford and Massinger were resigning the art which they had received,' &c. Massinger had been dead two years, he died in March 16$\frac{39}{40}$, and it is probable that Ford died about the same time. On page 11 it is confidently asserted that Philips's Cyder was written in 1699. Philips's Cyder was published in 1708, and all that is known about the time of its composition is that it was begun at Oxford and completed in the year before its publication. That the first book could not have been composed before 1705, and the second before 1706, is proved by internal evidence. In the first book there is an allusion to Harley being a member of Anne's Privy Council,. and Harley was sworn of the Privy Council in the spring of 1704. There is an allusion to the intense heat of the summer and autumn of 1705, and to the death of Miss Winchecombe,. Bolingbroke's sister-in-law, who died in the autumn of that year. In the second book there is an allusion to the consummation of the union between England and Scotland, the articles of which were signed in July 1706. So much for Mr. Gosse's assertion, that Philips's poem was written in 1699. On page 121 it is stated that Corneille's famous comedy, the Menteur, belongs to the year 1646. Corneille's Menteur was produced in 1642, and was first printed in October 1644. On page 237 we are informed that Dr. Allestree, the Provost of Eton, died in 1668. Dr. Allestree, the Provost of Eton,. died on the 28th of January, 168$\frac{8}{9}$. We are told on page 210,. that John Norris's Miscellanies were brought out in 1678. John Norris brought out his Miscellanies in 1687. Indeed, Mr. Gosse appears to be incapable of transcribing a date correctly, even when it must have been before his very eyes. On page

page 55, for example, he twice asserts that Waller's verses To
the King on his Navy were written in 1621, when the date
1626 is given under the title of the poem.   On page 84 we read,
' It was during the famous debate of February 8th, 1642, on the
Ecclesiastical Petitions that Waller seems to have made up his
mind to quit his party.'   The ' famous debate ' on the Ecclesiastical Petitions commenced on February 8th, 164⁹⁄₁.   We shall
not weary our readers by multiplying instances of these
blunders, for we have cited quite enough to show how far Mr.
Gosse's chronological statements are to be depended on.   But the
following is so exquisitely characteristic, not only of Mr. Gosse
himself but of the Dilettanti School generally, that we cannot
pass it by.   ' Late in the summer, one handsome and gallant
young fellow '—Mr. Gosse is speaking of the death of Sidney
Godolphin—' riding down the deep-leaved lanes that led from
Dartmoor . . . , met a party of Roundheads, was cut down and
killed ' (p. 109).   Now Sidney Godolphin was killed at the end
of January 164⅔, when the lanes were, we apprehend, not deep-
leaved; he was, it may be added, not handsome, for Clarendon
especially enlarges on the meanness of his person ; he was not
' cut down and killed,' he was shot dead by a musket ball ; he
was not meeting a party of Roundheads in the lanes, he was
pursuing them into Chagford.*

We are sorry to say that, bad as all this is, worse is to come.
Almost all Mr. Gosse's statements and generalizations, literary
and historical alike, are on a par with his chronology.   There
is not a chapter—nay, if we except the Appendices and index, it
would be difficult to find five consecutive pages which do not
swarm with errors and absurdities.   And the peculiarity of
Mr. Gosse's errors is, that they cannot be classed among those to
which even well-informed men are liable.   They are not mere
slips of the pen, they are not clerical and superficial, not such
as, casually arising, may be easily excised, but they are, to
borrow a metaphor from medicine, local manifestations of
constitutional mischief.   The ignorance which Mr. Gosse displays of the simplest facts of Literature and History is sufficiently extraordinary, but the recklessness with which he
exposes that ignorance transcends belief.   Will our readers
credit that Mr. Gosse attributes the pseudo-classicism of the
diction of the eighteenth-century poetry to the influence of the
writings of Anthony Ashley Cooper, first Earl of Shaftesbury ; †
that he asserts that ' it was Waller's duty to seize English

---

* Clarendon, 'History,' book vi.; *id.*, 'Life of Himself,' p. 24.
† Page 12 and Index.

Poetry

Poetry by the wings, and to shut it up in a cage for a hundred and fifty years'; * that Cleveland and Wild were the leaders of a reaction against the classical school; † and that he accounts for the fact, that it was Waller who 'revolutionized' poetry in England, and not Milton, 'because Milton was born three years later than Waller'? The latter part of this amazing nonsense we give in Mr. Gosse's own words:—

'Why was it not John Milton instead of Edmund Waller to whom it was given to revolutionize poetry in England? Here again, as everywhere, where we look closely into the historic development of literature, we see the value of dates and the paramount importance of a clear chronological sequence. Broadly speaking, it was because Milton was born three years later than Waller, and did not so rapidly come to maturity, that we did not receive from him a classical bias which would have been something very different from Waller's.' —Page 40.

We shall certainly not condescend to discuss such stuff as this. We may, however, remark, with regard to the assertion about Shaftesbury, that Mr. Gosse has of course confounded the Shaftesbury of the Cabal—the great Shaftesbury who was the first Earl—with the Shaftesbury of the Characteristics, who was the third Earl. And this is a University Lecturer! We need scarcely say that the Shaftesbury of the Characteristics was as guiltless of being the first to corrupt diction with the peculiar kind of classicism to which Mr. Gosse alludes, as the Shaftesbury of the Cabal. If Mr. Gosse were not ignorant of the very rudiments of the history of our prose literature, he would know that the style of which he is speaking was simply a phase of Euphuism, that it is abundantly illustrated in such well-known books as Howel's Familiar Letters, published in 1645, quarter of a century before Shaftesbury was born, and Urquhart's Jewel, published in 1652, and that it is to be found in full perfection, as Dunlop's extract shows, in the romance of Eliana, published nearly fifty years before the earliest of Shaftesbury's compositions saw the light.

But to proceed. What, in Mr. Gosse's opinion, constitutes one of Waller's chief claims to the honour of 'having revolutionized our poetry,' is the fact that he was the first who, in composing heroic couplets, terminated on principle the sense with the couplet. That Waller was writing in this style as early as 1621, is Mr. Gosse's grand discovery; and as a proof that Waller was writing in this style as early as 1621, Mr. Gosse

---

* Page 47.   † Pages 183–4.

characteristically

characteristically cites a poem written in or after 1626 ;* 'I shall show,' he says in another place, 'by irrefragable proof that Waller was writing didactic occasional poems in distichs which were often as good as Dryden's ever became'—he means, we presume, poems in which the proportion of distichs is as great as will be found in Dryden's poems—'as early as 1623' (p. 20).

Mr. Gosse does not seem to be aware that Johnson and others had made the same astounding discovery, though without drawing the same astounding conclusion. 'In his eighteenth year,' says Johnson, 'Waller wrote the poem On the Prince's Escape at St. Andero, a piece which justifies the observation made by one of his editors, that he attained by a felicity like instinct a style which will perhaps never be obsolete. His versification was, in his first essay, such as it appears in his last performance.'† Indeed, there is nothing in Mr. Gosse's volume more annoying than his habit of perpetually thrusting himself into prominence where there is no occasion for it. Who requires irrefragable proofs of dates and facts which no one questions, and which are to be found in so common a book as Johnson's Lives? There are probably not half-a-dozen well-read people in England who do not know that the famous lines in Denham's 'Cooper's Hill' beginning 'O could I flow like thee,' were added in the second edition. Indeed, they are the stock illustration of what Johnson calls 'felicitous afterthoughts.' Now hear Mr. Gosse, announcing another 'discovery'; 'There exists a mystery about these lines. In collating the first edition I was amazed to find them absent, and they do not occur,'‡ &c. A very offensive instance of the same kind of thing may be found on pp. 159–60. Speaking of a certain well-known pamphlet relating to 'Gondibert,'—'Certain verses written by several of the author's friends to be reprinted with the second edition of "Gondibert," '—Mr. Gosse says, referring to its authorship, 'I believe that I detect Denham, Cleveland, the younger Donne, and Jasper Mayne, as the wicked anonymous quartet;' adding, in a note, 'After forming this conjecture,

---

* Page 55. The poém which Mr. Gosse cites is the poem to the 'King on his Navy,' which was certainly not written before 1626, and may, as Fenton supposes, have been written as late as 1635; but the poem to which he means to allude is no doubt the verses on His Majesty's escape in the Road at St. Andero, which one editor dates 1621, but which could not have been written before the autumn of 1623, as the event to which they refer occurred either at the end of September or the beginning of October in that year.

† 'Life of Waller.'

‡ Among many other places where this had been pointed out, it may suffice to specify the following; Spence's 'Anecdotes' (Singer's edit.), p. 213. Malone, 'Prose Works of Dryden,' vol. iv. p. 521, *note*. Johnson's 'Lives of the Poets' (Cunningham's edition), vol. i. p. 78. Moore's 'Life of Byron,' vol. ii. p. 193. Chalmers's 'Biog. Dict.,' art. Denham.' Campbell's 'Specimens,' ed. 1841, p. 244.

I discovered,

I discovered, in a copy of the 1653 pamphlet in the Library of Yale College a MS. note suggesting that the four authors were Denham, the younger Donne, Sir Allen Broderick, and William Crofts.' Now Mr. Gosse must have been perfectly aware that what he 'detected' and 'discovered' had been long ago detected and discovered by Isaac Disraeli in a work as well known as any work in the English language. 'It is said,' observes Disraeli, referring to this tract, 'that there were four writers, probably Sir John Denham and Jo. Donne, Sir Allen Broderick and Will Crofts.' * A still more offensive illustration of this officious egotism will be found on page 243. If there is any fact in biographical chronology which has never been disputed, it is that Denham died in March 166⅚. That date was entered, and may still, of course, be seen, in the register at the Abbey; it is given correctly by Anthony Wood, by Johnson, by Chalmers; it is, with two exceptions, given correctly in every biographical dictionary, in every encyclopædia, in every manual of English Literature which we have consulted. But in the 'Biographia Britannica,' 1688 chances, by a mere clerical error, to be substituted for 1668. This gives Mr. Gosse an opportunity for displaying his knowledge of 'contemporary records'—these 'contemporary records' dwindling somewhat ignominiously into two or three extracts from 'Pepys's Diary:' 'In many text-books,' he begins by observing, 'the date of Denham's death is given as 1688. But this seems highly improbable. From contemporary records I have collected a few dates,' &c. . . . 'On the 21st of February, 1665, Pepys dined with Denham, who was evidently perfectly well. . . . In the early part of 1666 the Duke of York's attentions to Lady Denham became marked; in the summer she yields to them, and Denham becomes mad. In 1668 Pepys hears a rumour of his death, which rumour may or may not be true, but has no doubt introduced that date into the text-books.' And so on. It was this rumour, we presume, which accounts for the entry of Denham's burial in the register at the Abbey, a reference to which would have saved us from all this 'skimble skamble stuff' about contemporary records, rumours and text-books.

But these are trifles. We return to Mr. Gosse's grand discovery, that we owe to Waller 'the first experiment in distich' (p. 40); that Waller was, that is to say, the first who in composing the heroic couplet 'concluded the sense in the couplet,' and that he was writing in distichs in 1621, nearly quarter of a century before any one else in England was doing so' (p. 55). No more absurd statement was ever made. Before 1557 Nicholas Grimoald was thus writing heroic couplets:—

---

* 'Calamities and Quarrels of Authors' (Popular Edition), p. 409.

'In

> ' In mean is virtue plac'd ; on either side,
>   Both right and left, amiss a man may slide.
>   Icar, with fire hadst thou the midway flown,
>   Icarian beck by name had no man known.
>   If middle path had kept proud Phaeton
>   Ne burning brand this earth had fallen upon.
>   Ne cruel power, ne none so soft can reign,
>   That keeps a mean the same shall still maintain.'

And so on through the whole poem.*

Before 1593 Robert Greene was thus habitually writing heroic couplets :—

> ' Most gracious King,—that they that little prove
>   Are mickle blest from bitter sweets of love.
>   And well I wot I heard a shepherd sing,
>   That like a bee, Love hath a little sting ;
>   He lurks in flowers, he percheth on the trees,
>   He on king's pillows bends his pretty knees.
>   The boy is blind, but when he will not spy,
>   He hath a leaden foot and wings to fly.' †

Before 1597 Hall was thus writing :—

> ' Their royal plate was clay, or wood, or stone ;
>   The vulgar, save his hand, else had he none.
>   Their only cellar was the neighbour brook ;
>   None did for better care, for better look.
>   Was then no plaining of the brewer's scape,
>   Nor greedy vintner mix'd the strainèd grape.
>   The King's pavilion was the grassy green
>   Under safe shelter of the shady treen.
>   Under each bank men laid their limbs along,
>   Not wishing any ease, not fearing wrong.' ‡

And so habitually does Hall confine the sense to the couplet, that of the forty couplets of which the ' Satire' from which we have quoted is composed, there are only two in which the second line flows over into the first line of the following couplet. At least ten years before Waller had published a line, George Sandys was writing heroic couplets simply undistinguishable from Pope's couplets, of which these are the type :—

> ' Our graver Muse from her long dream awakes,
>   Peneian groves and Cirrha's caves forsakes ;
>   Inspir'd with zeal, she climbs th' etherial hills
>   Of Solyma, where bleeding balm distills ;
>   Where trees of life unfading youth assure,
>   And living waters all diseases cure.'

---

* ' Praise of Measure keeping,' (published in Tottel's ' Miscellany,' 1557).
† 'James IV.,' act i. sc. 1.
‡ Hall's ' Satires,' Sat. 1, Bk. iii. (published in 1597).

But

But we need go no further than page 246 to show how utterly erroneous, how incredibly reckless Mr. Gosse's assertions are. He there observes that 'Herrick for once in his life, merely because he had been reading Cooper's Hill, writes in excellent distichs;' and he then proceeds to quote six lines, adding, 'No one would suspect that these lines were written by the song-bird of the Hesperides.' Why, the very opening lines of the 'Hesperides' are composed in distichs as correct and smooth as Pope's, in distichs infinitely more musical than Waller ever wrote:—

> 'I sing of brooks, of blossoms, birds and bowers,
> Of April, May, of June, and July flowers.
> I sing of maypoles, hock carts, wassails, wakes,
> Of bridegrooms, brides, and of their bridal cakes.
>
> * * * * *
>
> I sing of dewes and rains, and, piece by piece,
> Of balm, of oil, of spice and ambergreece.
> I sing of times trans-shifting; and I write
> How roses first came red, and lilies white.'

And distichs as finished as these are to be found by hundreds in Herrick's poems. After this, our readers will probably not be surprised to hear, on Mr. Gosse's authority, that 'the dactylic and anapæstic movement was, curiously enough, entirely unknown to the Elizabethans' (p. 10). It would, however, be interesting to know how he scans such verses as Tusser's:—

> 'God sendeth and giveth both mouth and the meat,
> And blesseth us all with his benefits great.
> Then serve we the God who so richly doth give,
> Shew love to our neighbours, and lay for to live,' &c.

And such verses abound in Tusser.
Or Heywood's:—

> 'Now woe with the willow and woe with the wight,
> That windeth willow, willow garland to dight;
> That dole dealt in allmesse is all amiss quite,
> Where lovers are beggars for allmesse in sight,' &c.

Or Jonson's:—

> 'My masters and friends and good people draw near,
> And look to your purses for that I do say,' &c.

Or the song attributed to Lyly:—

> 'Round about, round about in a fine ring-a,
> Thus we dance, thus we dance and thus we sing-a,
> Trip and go, to and fro, over this green-a,
> All about, in and out, for our brave Queen-a.'

Or Fletcher's :—

> ' Come, Fortune's a jade, I care not who tell her,
> Would offer to strangle a page of the cellar ;
> But thus she does still, when she pleases to palter,
> Instead of his wages she gives him a halter.'

The truth of course is, that the dactylic and anapæstic rhythm, though rarely used in serious poetry, was habitually used by the Elizabethan writers in semi-serious and comic poetry.

On page 165 we find the following amazing statement. Speaking of Dryden's employment of the heroic quatrain in the Annus Mirabilis (1667), Mr. Gosse goes on to inform us, that the heroic quatrain ' was not again employed all through the Restoration or the Augustan age, nor again until, in 1743, the Earl of Chesterfield brought out the posthumous Elegies of his young cousin Hammond.' The heroic quatrain was employed habitually by poets between 1667 and 1743. It was employed by Aphra Behn ; it was employed by Blackmore ; it was employed by Wycherley, by Sheffield, by Walsh, by Garth, by Prior, by Swift, by Hughes, by Rowe, by Gay, not reckoning the continuation of Gondibert, which is probably not genuine ; it was employed by Pope, by Parnell, by Savage, by Aaron Hill.

But this is nothing to what follows. Our readers will probably believe us to be jesting when we inform them that Mr. Gosse deliberately asserts, that between 1660 and ' about 1760 ' Milton and Roscommon were the only poets who employed blank verse :—

> ' From 1660 onwards to about 1760 the exact opposite was the case (that is, that the couplet superseded blank verse). A poet of decent abilities was sure of readers if he would write in the couplet.' Then, in a note, he adds : ' Milton would stand absolutely alone in his preference of another form if Roscommon, also in 1684, in emulation of " Paradise Lost," had not chosen to throw off what he calls the restraint of Rime in his Art of Poetry.'

Has Mr. Gosse ever inspected the All for Love and the Don Sebastian of Dryden ; the Mourning Bride of Congreve ; the Julius Cæsar of Sheffield ; the blank verse tragedies of Crowne ; the later dramas of Davenant ; the tragedies of Otway, Lee, Southern, Rowe, Lillo, and Thomson ; Addison's tragedy of Cato ; Smith's tragedy of Hippolytus ; Hughes's Siege of Damascus ; Johnson's Irene ? Has he ever read Roscommon's own parody of Milton, inserted in the Essay on Translated Verse ; or Addison's Ovidian translation in Miltonic verse ;

or

or Lady Winchelsea's Fanscomb Barn; or Philips's Splendid Shilling, Blenheim, and Cyder; or Aaron Hill's Cleon to Lycidas? Can he be unaware that within those years were published Thomson's Seasons and Liberty; Dyer's Ruins of Rome, and Fleece; Akenside's Pleasures of Imagination; Armstrong's Art of Preserving Health; Somerville's Chace, and Hobbinol; Glover's Leonidas, Mallet's Excursion, Blair's Grave, Young's Night Thoughts, not to speak of innumerable other poems less celebrated?

Nor is Mr. Gosse more to be depended on when he favours us with remarks on Italian literature. We give one specimen:—

'A sort of classical revival was attempted at the close of the sixteenth century by Chiabrera, who, in disdaining the folly of Marinists and in trying to recall his countrymen to a Greek simplicity, attained a position somewhat analogous to that of Cowley. But he stood alone until Filicaja came.'—Page 15.

The impression which such statements as these must produce on a reader who knows anything of the poetry of Chiabrera and his contemporaries and successors, it would be difficult to describe. No mere enumeration of positive blunders could convey any idea of its absurdity. It may, however, be sufficient to say, that two-thirds of Chiabrera's most characteristic poems were published before Marini had given a line to the world; that, so far from Chiabrera standing alone, he was the master of a flourishing school of disciples and imitators, and of such disciples and imitators as Fulvio Testi, Virginio Cesarini, and Giovanni Ciampoli; and that, so far from recalling his countrymen to 'Greek simplicity'—whatever that may mean—he was not only an imitator of Pindar, but out-Pindared Pindar in the elaborate pomp, and studied artificiality of his diction.

But the recklessness with which Mr. Gosse displays his ignorance of the very elements of literature is, if possible, exceeded by the recklessness with which he displays his ignorance of the commonest facts of history and biography. We will give one or two examples. In the life of Waller, Mr. Gosse finds this sentence: 'Mr. Saville used to say that no man in England should keep him company without drinking but Ned Waller.' This becomes, in Mr. Gosse's narrative, 'George Savile, Lord Halifax, the famous *viveur*, and a pupil of Waller's, in verse, said,' &c. (p. 236). It would be difficult to match this. Nearly every word is a blunder. Indeed, we will boldly say that, if our own or any other literature were ransacked, it would be ransacked in vain for a sentence which

condenses

condenses so many errors and so much of that *crassa negligentia*, which is as reprehensible in writers as it is in lawyers and doctors. George Savile, Lord Halifax, who is apparently known only to Mr. Gosse as 'the famous *viveur*,' was, as we need scarcely say, one of the most distinguished statesmen of the seventeenth century. He was in no sense of the word a *viveur*. He was not a pupil of Waller. He never, so far as is recorded, wrote a line of verse in his life. But there was another Lord Halifax, who might perhaps be known to Mr. Gosse only in connection with his convivial habits and his bad poetry, but who is known to everyone else as the Originator of the National Debt, as the Founder of the Bank of England, and as the most eminent financier in English history. It is this Lord Halifax who might, as the author of a copy of verses on the death of Charles II., be described as a pupil of Waller. And it is of this Lord Halifax that Mr. Gosse is probably thinking. But the name of this Lord Halifax was, unfortunately for Mr. Gosse, Charles Montague. The 'Mr. Savile' alluded to, was in truth neither George Savile, Marquis of Halifax, nor Charles Montague, Earl of Halifax, but Henry Savile a younger son of Sir William Savile, and a younger brother of the Marquis.

'When the Queen fled from Exeter,' says Mr. Gosse, 'with the new-born Princess of Wales in July 1644' (p. 113). If Mr. Gosse had consulted his 'eminent friend,' Professor Gardiner, he would have learned that the younger daughters of English Kings are not Princesses of Wales ; and as he appears to be fond of picturesque touches, he might, had he pushed his enquiries, have ascertained that to this particular child a peculiar interest is attached. If too, when writing the lines which follow, he had taken the trouble to turn to the Biographia Britannica, he would have discovered that 'the young Duke of Newcastle,' who 'fled from defeat at Marston Moor,' was in his fifty-third year, and that he was, moreover, not a Duke, but a Marquis.

We proceed to something much more serious. To the historian of Literature nothing should be so sacred as the reputation of the Dead, and on no point is he bound in honour to be more sensitively scrupulous than when he is called upon to discuss anything which may reflect unfavourably on that reputation. Now on the same page (p. 113), we find a statement which, unless Mr. Gosse is prepared to produce his authority for it, we do not scruple to designate a gross and shameful libel on the memory of as worthy a man as ever lived, 'James Shirley, who had left a starving wife and children behind him, was in attendance (at Paris) upon his Royal Mistress.' This is repeated

on

on pp. 117, 118. Speaking of the 'balls, comedies and prome-nades,' with which 'the English exiles were regaled at Fontaine-bleau,' in 1646 and 1647, Mr. Gosse says that Shirley was 'certainly' present at them, Waller and Hobbes probably, but Shirley 'certainly.' Now our only authority for the life of Shirley is Anthony Wood, and what Wood says is this:—'When the rebellion broke out Shirley was invited by his patron, Newcastle, to attend him in the war.' This Shirley appears to have done. But after the King's cause declined—we give Wood's own words—'he, following his old trade of teaching, not only gained a comfortable subsistence, but educated many ingenious youths, who afterwards proved most eminent in divers faculties.' In this honourable drudgery, undertaken for the support of his wife and children, all Shirley's life between about 1644 and 1660, appears to have been passed, and his conduct has elicited just praise from his biographers. If Mr. Gosse is in possession of documents hitherto unknown, it was his duty to have specified them, and it is his duty to produce them. Till he does so we shall continue to believe that this is only one of his many other loose and random assertions, and to protest against such unwarrantable liberties being taken with the biographies of eminent men.

We have by no means exhausted the list of Mr. Gosse's blunders, but we have, we fear, exhausted the patience of our readers. What further remarks, therefore, we have to make shall be brief. We have given a few specimens of Mr. Gosse's method of dealing with facts ; we will now give a few specimens of his criticism. That excellent man, Mr. Pecksniff, was, we are told, in the habit of using any word that occurred to him as having a fine sound, and rounding a sentence well, without much care for its meaning, 'and this,' says his biographer, 'he did so boldly and in such an imposing manner, that he would sometimes stagger the wisest people, and make them gasp again.' This is precisely Mr. Gosse's method. About the propriety of his epithets, so long as they sound well, he never troubles himself; sometimes they are so vague as to mean anything, sometimes they have no meaning at all, as often they are inconsistent with each other. What is predicated of a work in one place is directly contradicted in another. Thus (p. 34), Drayton's Barons' Wars is described as 'a serene and lovely poem;' on the very next page we are told that a 'passionate music runs through it;' and on page 75 this same 'serene and lovely poem' is described as 'possessing various brilliant and touching qualities, irregular force, and sudden brilliance of style.' Thus, on page 158, Davenant's Gondibert, coupled with Southey's Epics, is compared to 'a

vast

vast sapless trunk, one of the largest trees in girth and height, but the deadest of them all, with scarcely a cluster of green buds here and there;' at the bottom of the same page we are told that it owed its popularity 'to its gorgeous and exotic imagery.' On page 121, the versification of Dryden is distinguished by its 'sullen majesty;' Denham's lines on the Thames are 'marvellous;' Horace's Ars Poetica is a 'wonderful prelude.' Milton and Crashaw 'sanctified the rainbow fancies of the Marinist School by hallowing them to sacred uses' (p. 172). Fulke Greville, whose cramped, condensed and elliptic style has, as we need scarcely say, passed into a proverb, possesses 'the old Sidneian sweetness.' Pope's Dunciad is 'admirable for its facility of construction.' On page 71, a battle between the islanders of Bermuda 'and two spermaceti whales that had got stranded in a shallow bay,' is 'a sort of pseudo-Homeric subject.' Mr. Gosse's observations are, it may be added, never so amusing as when he touches on points of classical learning, and the extraordinary self-complacency with which they are enunciated, adds to their absurdity. 'When a young fellow,' he says, 'prefers Moschus to Homer, and Ausonius to Virgil, we know how to class him.' Whether such a young fellow has ever existed, or if he does exist, whether he is worth classing at all, is probably a reflection which will occur to most people. But when a young fellow, or an old fellow, talks of 'the grace of Latinity' (p. 11), or tells us that it was the property of hellebore to produce forgetfulness (p. 46), or informs us that Aristotle and Horace have left rules for the composition of a 'straightforward prosaic poetry' (p. 38), it is not, we apprehend, very difficult to class him.*

Mr. Gosse, in paying an obscure dramatist the compliment of quoting him, tells us that he felt as though the ghost of the poet whom he had thus honoured 'might be breathing hard by his side at the excitement of resuscitation.' We are inclined to think that if the ghosts of Macaulay and Spedding could have rambled into the old beloved Hall during the delivery of these lectures, Mr. Gosse might have heard them also 'breathing hard,' not 'at the excitement of resuscitation,' but in excitement, having its origin from a very different cause.

If we turn from the matter of Mr. Gosse's volume to the style

---

* It is a great misfortune to Mr. Gosse that his work cannot be estimated by the Index, which, to do him justice, is a model of its kind. But it is a very Barmecide Feast. Under the heading, for example, of Aristotle, we find 'Aristotle's rules for composition,' but on referring to the page indicated—page 38—for those rules, we are concerned to see them dwindling down to the insignificant proportions of the short clause we have just quoted.

and the diction, it is equally surprising that any University could have sanctioned its publication. How even the reader for the press could have allowed such words as 'preciosity,' 'recrudescence,' 'solidarity,' 'rejuvenescence,' 'alembicated,' or such phrases as 'the lively actuality of a newsletter,' 'a personal sympathy with vegetation,' 'the excitement of resuscitation,' and the like, to pass unchallenged, is to us inexplicable. Was there no one who could save Mr. Gosse from making himself ridiculous by such eloquence as this : 'We who can see this Orpheus-like Charles torn to pieces by the outraged liberties of England, and that comely head floating down the Hebrus of the Revolution'?—(p. 81). Could the Delegates of the Cambridge Press have been blind to the ludicrous impropriety of permitting what was intended to be a serious treatise on English Literature to be prefaced by a copy of silly verses, in which the author—an official of the University—assures his readers that he is—

> 'Less than bird or shell,
> More volatile, more fragile far than these.'

Nor does the bad taste—to call it by no harsher name—which is conspicuous throughout the book, less jar on us. Speaking, for example, of Waller's Battle of the Summer Islands, Mr. Gosse observes, 'My own belief is that the astute Waller, having property on the Islands, wrote his heroic poem and circulated it among wealthy and noble friends as an advertisement.' Can Mr. Gosse possibly be ignorant that Waller was a gentleman? So again, when he talks of the 'tattling monkey-tongue' of Pope, we have an example of one of the most detestable fashions of modern times—we mean the pert irreverence with which very little men are in the habit of speaking of great men.

And now we bring to a conclusion one of the most disagreeable tasks which it has ever been our lot to undertake. Our motives for undertaking it have already been explained. Had Mr. Gosse's volume been published in the ordinary way, we need scarcely say that we should not have noticed it. Had its errors and deficiencies been pointed out in the literary journals, we should probably have comforted ourselves with the thought, that what had been done once need not be done again. But when we saw that it came forth, carrying all the authority of a work published by a great University, and under the auspices of the most distinguished community in that University, and that so far from the literary journals estimating it at its true value, and placing students on their guard against its errors, Review vied with Review in fulsome and indiscriminating

nating eulogy,* we felt we had no choice. It was simply our duty, our imperative duty, in the interests of literature and in the interests of education, to speak out. That duty we have endeavoured to perform temperately and candidly. We have perverted nothing. We have coloured nothing. Had it been our object to make game of the book, it would not, we can assure Mr. Gosse, have been very difficult. Though we have, we own, been strongly tempted to comment as severely on his delinquencies as they certainly deserve, we have deliberately forborne. We have even refrained from discussing matters of opinion. We have confined ourselves entirely to matters of fact—to gross and palpable blunders, to unfounded and reckless assertions, to such absurdities in criticism and such vices of style as will in the eyes of discerning readers carry with them their own condemnation. When we consider the circulation secured to this volume from the mere fact of its having issued from so famous a press, and under such distinguished patronage, it is melancholy to think of the errors to which it will give currency. We only hope that our exposure of them will have the effect of serving in some degree to counteract the mischief.

Now the Universities must know, or ought to know, that this kind of thing will not do. If they are resolved to encourage the study of English Literature, it is their duty to see that it is studied properly. If it is not studied properly, the sooner they cease to profess to study it the better. No good can possibly come from Dilettantism. No good can possibly come from unskilled teaching. To tolerate either is to defeat the purposes for which the Universities are designed, is to initiate corruption which will inevitably spread, is to establish precedents which time will confirm. We have already pointed out the responsibility which rests with the centres of education in days like these, and it is, therefore, with just alarm that we find them countenancing, in any subject represented by them, such work as the work on which we have been animadverting.

But whatever be the faults of Mr. Gosse's book, it will not, we hope, be without its use. If it illustrates comprehensively the manner in which English literature should not be taught, it may, on the 'lucus a non lucendo' principle, direct attention to the manner in which it should be taught, and on that subject

---

* One of our leading literary journals terminated a review which, though extending to six columns, did not point out a single error, with these words : ' It is a volume not to be glanced over and thrown aside, and we recommend the student of English Poetry to read it twice and consult it often.' Such is sometimes the value of 'review' advertisements.

we

we propose to make a few remarks. The first fact which the Universities ought to recognize is, that a literature, which is represented by such poets as Shakespeare and Milton, as Pope and Wordsworth, and by such prose writers as Bacon and Hooker, as Gibbon and Burke, is a very serious thing, much too serious a thing to be abandoned either to unskilled teachers or to philologists ; that it is a literature not inferior in intrinsic merit to the literatures of the Ancient World, that it is, therefore, from an historical point of view, worthy of minute, of patient, of systematic study ; and that, regarded as an instrument of culture, it is—if studied in a liberal and enlightened spirit—of the utmost value and importance. But of this, to judge from such books as Mr. Gosse's on the one hand, and by such editions of the English classics as the Clarendon Press provides on the other hand, the Universities appear at present to have no conception. We are very far from wishing to speak disrespectfully of the Clarendon Press publications, for they are, so far as they go, sound and thorough—the work, as a rule, of accurate and painstaking scholars. But their radical defect lies in the fact, that they do not sufficiently distinguish between philology and literature. Instead of regarding a great poem or a great drama as the expression of genius and art, they appear to regard it merely as a monument of language. They dwell with tedious and unnecessary minuteness on points which can interest none but grammarians and philologists, and out of this narrow sphere they seldom or never travel, unless perhaps to explain some historical allusion, to discuss some problem in antiquities, or to accumulate wholly superfluous parallel passages. In the Clarendon Press edition of Milton, for example, nothing is so common as to find a quarter of a page of notes, of which the following is a sample :

‘1. 619. Cp. Ovid, ‘Metamorphoses,’ xi. 419 ; ‘Faery Queen,’ 1, xi. 4.

1. 624. Cp. Ovid, ‘Metamorphoses,’ ix. 6.

1. 630. Cp. Horace, ‘Odes,’ iii. 2, 17.

1. 633. Cp. ‘Paradise Lost,’ ii. 692 ; v. 710 ; vi. 156 ; Rev. xii. 4.

1. 642. *tempted our attempt.* Keightley claims to have been the first to point out that these plays upon words are imitations of the Paronomasia in Scripture. Cf. v. 869 ; ix. 11 ; xii. 78.

1. 659. ‘Iliad,’ i. 140.

1. 660. *peace is despair'd*, a Latinism. So ‘despair thy charm,’ Macbeth, v. 7.

No one could say of the author of notes like these that he displays either want of industry or want of learning, but such

notes

notes are, from an educational point of view, all but useless;
they are even worse; they render what should be an agreeable
and profitable study, simply repulsive. They serve no end;
they satisfy no need. It is on this ground, therefore, that we
think the Clarendon Press series unsatisfactory. They err not
on the side of superficiality or on the side of crude and imperfect learning, but on the side of too narrow a conception of
the scope and method of interpreting literature; they err, in
short, as Pope taunted Kuster and Burmann with erring:

> ' The critic eye, that microscope of wit,
>   Sees hairs and pores, examines bit by bit,'

but fails to see

> ' How parts relate to parts, or they to whole,
>   The body's harmony, the beaming soul.'

That pedantry is, when allied with learning, a far less evil
than dilettantism, no one would dispute. Such a study of the
English Classics as the Clarendon Press editors prescribe, is
not, indeed, calculated either to enlarge a youth's mind or to
refine his taste; it is still less calculated to awaken rational
curiosity, or to inspire a love of literature for its own sake; but,
regarded as a mode of discipline, it may possibly, in some
cases, be of service in forming and confirming habits of accuracy,
and, within certain limits, habits of thoroughness, and in
training and strengthening the memory. But this cannot be
pleaded in favour of dilettantism. Of all the pests that beset
and impede culture, dilettantism is by far the most mischievous.
It is to real learning precisely what the phantom sent by Juno
to deceive Turnus was to the real Æneas. It assumes its form;
it brandishes what seem to be its weapons; it mimics its gait;
it simulates its speech. But it is a mockery and a fraud. It
serves only to delude and mislead. Nor is this all. It is not
simply an intellectual, but a moral evil. It encourages those
lazy and desultory habits into which young students are
especially prone to fall. It tends to render them indifferent to
the distinction between accuracy and inaccuracy, between truth
and falsehood. It emasculates, it corrupts, it strikes at the
very root of that conscientiousness and honesty, that absolute
sincerity, which is, or ought to be, the first article in the creed
of every scholar and of every teacher.

But the time will, we trust, come when Oxford and
Cambridge will see the necessity of raising the study of our
national literature to its proper level in education, and when
neither dilettantism nor pedantry will be permitted to stand
in the way of that study. But before that can be done, they

must

must recognize the distinction between philology and literature, between the significance of the 'Literæ Humaniores' as interpreted by verbal critics, and their significance as interpreted by such critics as Lessing and Coleridge. They must think less of the letter and more of the spirit. They must cease to dwell solely on what is accidental, and see the necessity for penetrating to the essence which is the life. Philological criticism is to criticism, in the proper sense of the term, what anatomy is to psychology. Each has its importance, each is in a manner related, and each should be studied, but who would dream of confounding them? The scalpel, which lays bare every nerve and every artery in the mechanism of the body, reveals nothing further. The Agamemnon and Macbeth are as little likely to yield up the secret of their life to the verbal scholar.

Much has recently been talked about the continuity of history, and the erroneous views which must necessarily result from studying it piecemeal. The continuity of literature is a fact of even more importance, and the persistency with which that fact has been ignored has not only led to errors infinitely more serious than any which can be imputed to historical teachers, but has rendered our whole system of dealing with literature, whether historically, in tracing its development, or critically, in analysing its phenomena, as inadequate as it is unsound. One of the most remarkable illustrations of this is the fact, that the study of our own literature is, in all our schools and colleges, separated on principle from the study of the literatures of Greece and Rome. Its teachers are, as a rule, men who make no pretension to classical learning, or, if they possess it, never dream of applying it to the interpretation of English. Not long ago an eminent London publisher announced a series of annotated English Classics, one of the chief attractions of which was that it was to be edited by 'none but men who had made a special study of their mother tongue,' as 'the belief that a knowledge of Greek and Latin was a qualification for editing English authors was,' so ran the prospectus—'a belief which the projectors of the series did not share.' Now the literatures of Greece, Rome, and England, are radically and essentially connected. What the literature of Greece is to that of Rome, the literatures of Greece and Rome are to that of England. A scholar would at once see the absurdity of separating the study of Roman literature from the study of Greek literature, for the simple reason, that without a knowledge of the latter the former is unintelligible. We wonder what would be thought of a man who should profess to interpret the

Æneid

Æneid without possessing an adequate acquaintance with the
Homeric Poems, with the Attic Drama, with the poetry of
Alexandria; or of a man who set up to expound the Odes of
Horace, or to comment on the style of Sallust and Tacitus, who
was ignorant of Greek lyric poetry and of Thucydides. We
wonder what would be the fate of an editor of the Georgics
who knew nothing of the Works and Days; of an editor of the
Bucolics, who knew nothing of the Sicilian Idylls; or of an
editor of Terence, who knew nothing of the New Comedy.

The absurdity of separating the study of our own classics
from the study of the classics of Greece and Rome is equally
great. Not only have most of our poets and all our best prose
writers, as well in the present age as in former ages, been
nourished on the literature of Greece and Rome; not only have
the forms of at least two-thirds of our best poetry and of our best
prose derived their distinctive features from those literatures;
not only has the influence of those literatures, alternately modi-
fying and moulding our own, determined its course and its
characteristics; but a large portion of what is most valuable in
our poetry is as historically unintelligible, apart from the Greek
and Roman Classics, as the Epic and Lyric Poetry of Rome
would be apart from the Epic and Lyric Poetry of Greece.
Take, for example, the poetry of Milton. It would not be too
much to say, that the literature of antiquity was to Milton's
genius what soil and light are to a plant. It nourished, it
coloured, it developed it. It determined not merely his character as an artist, but it exercised an influence on his intellect
and temper scarcely less powerful than hereditary instincts and
contemporary history. It at once animated and chastened his
imagination; it modified his fancy; it furnished him with his
models. On it his taste was formed; on it his style was
moulded. From it his diction and his method derived their
peculiarities. It transformed what would in all probability
have been the mere counterpart of Cædmon's Paraphrase or
Langland's Vision into Paradise Lost; and what would have
been the mere counterpart of Corydon's Doleful Knell, and the
satire of the Three Estates, into Lycidas and Comus. The
poetry of Gray, again, can only be fully appreciated, can only, in
the proper sense of the term, be understood by those who are
familiar with the literatures from which its characteristics and
its inspiration are derived. And what is true of the poetry of
Milton and Gray is true of the poetry of innumerable others.
There is much in the very essence of Spenser's poetry, there is
much in the very essence of Wordsworth's poetry, which must
be absolutely without meaning to readers ignorant of the
                                                    Platonic

Platonic philosophy, to readers ignorant of the Phædrus and the Phædo. Indeed the whole history of our early literature is little less than the history of the modification of Teutonic and Celtic elements by classical influences, as the history of the later development of that literature is the history of the alternate predominance of Classicism and Romanticism. It was the Roman drama, slightly modified by the Italian playwrights of the Renaissance, which determined the form of our Romantic drama. On the epics of Greece and Rome are modelled our own epics. Almost all our didactic poetry is professedly modelled on the didactic poetry of Rome. One important branch of our lyric poetry springs directly from Pindar; another important branch directly from Horace; another again directly from the Choral Odes of the Attic dramatists and Seneca. Our heroic satire, from Hall to Byron, is simply the counterpart, often indeed a mere imitation, of Roman satire. The Epistles which fill so large a space in the poetical literature of the seventeenth and eighteenth centuries derived their origin from those of Horace. To the Heroides of Ovid we owe a whole series of important poems. From them Chaucer borrowed the material for the most delightful of his minor works; on them Drayton modelled his Heroical Epistles, and Pope his Eloisa to Abelard. The tone, the style, the method, of such narratives as Beaumont's Bosworth Field and Addison's Campaign, themselves the subject of numberless imitations, are borrowed unmistakably from Lucan. Martial and the Anthology have furnished the archetypes of our epigrams and our epitaphs, and Theocritus and Virgil the archetypes of our Pastorals. Of our Elegiac poetry, to employ the term in its conventional sense, one portion is largely indebted to Theocritus, Moschus, and Virgil, and another portion still more largely indebted to Catullus and Ovid, to Tibullus and Propertius. Indeed it would be no exaggeration to say, that if the influence individually exercised by each of the Greek and Latin poets, we do not say of the first but of the second order, on our own poets were fully traced, each would afford ample matter for a bulky treatise.

But if this is the case with our poetry, how much more strikingly is it the case with our prose! No one can appreciate more than we do the sweetness, the simplicity, the grace of such prose as Maundeville's, as Malory's, as Bunyan's; and that our language would, had it pursued its course unmodified by classical influences, have been fully equal to the production of such prose, is all but certain. But Maundeville, Malory, and Bunyan, are not the names which rise to our lips when we speak
of

of the masters of prose expression. The history of English eloquence commences from the moment when the Roman Classics moulded and coloured our style—when periodic prose modelled itself on Cicero and Livy, when analytic prose modelled itself on Sallust and Tacitus. From Hooker to Milton, from Milton to Bolingbroke, and from Bolingbroke to Burke, this has been the case. The structure of their periods— allowing, of course, for differences of idiom—the evolution of their periods, their rhythm, their colouring, their tone are, when they rise to eloquence, precisely those of rhetorical Roman prose. It is commonly supposed that when, during the latter half of the seventeenth century, the long sentence began to be broken up, and the style which Addison and his school subsequently perfected became fashionable, the change is to be attributed to the influence of French writers. Nothing could be more erroneous. The style of Hobbes, Sprat, and Cowley, the style subsequently of Dryden and Temple, is as Latin as that of Hooker and Milton ; but with a difference. Instead of going to the diction of Livy and to the rhetorical works of Cicero for their models, they went to Quintilian, to the Younger Pliny, and to Cicero's colloquial and epistolary writings. And what is true of them is true of Addison. The serious style of Addison is modelled, as closely as any style could be, on that of the De Senectute and the De Amicitiâ.*

---

* This is an interesting question, and as our opinion may appear paradoxical, we will place side by side what will be allowed to be a typical sample of Cicero's literary style, and what will be allowed to be a typical sample of Addison's style. And the truth of what we have asserted will, we think, be at once apparent.

'Equidem non video cur quid ipse sentiam de morte non audeam vobis dicere ; quod eo melius mihi cernere videor quo ab eâ proprius absum. Ego vestros patres, P. Scipio, tuque C. Laeli, viros clarissimos mihique amicissimos, vivere arbitror, et eam quidem vitam, quae est sola vita nominanda. Nam dum sumus in his inclusi compagibus corporis munere quodam necessitatis et gravi opere perfungimur. Est enim animus coelestis ex altissimo domicilio depressus et quasi demersus in terram, locum divinae naturae aeternitatique contrarium. Sed credo Deos immortales sparsisse animos in corpora humana, ut essent qui terras tuerentur quique coelestium ordinem contemplantes imitarentur eum vitae modo atque constantiâ. Nec me solum ratio ac disputatio impulit ut ita crederem, sed nobilitas etiam summorum philosophorum et auctoritas.'—'De Senectute,' xxi.

'I know but one way of fortifying myself against these gloomy presages and terrors of mind, and that is by securing to myself the friendship and protection of that Being who is the disposer of events and governs futurity. He sees at one view the whole thread of my existence, not only that part which I have already passed through, but that which runs forward into all the depths of eternity. When I lay me down to sleep, I recommend myself to His care ; when I awake, I give myself up to His direction. Amidst all the evils which surround me, I will look up to Him for help and question, not that He will either avert them or turn them to my advantage. Though I know neither the time nor the manner of the death I am to die, I am not at all solicitous about it, because I am sure that He knows them both, and that He will not fail to comfort and support me under them.'—'Spectator,' p. 7.

It

It was the influence partly perhaps of Machiavelli and Guicciardini, but it was the influence mainly of Thucydides and Sallust, of Livy and Tacitus, which revolutionized our historical composition, which gave us Bacon for Capgrave, and Knolles and Herbert for Fabyan, and which was to determine the form, tone, and style of the great works which are the glory of our historic literature—of the great work of Clarendon in the seventeenth century; of the great works of Robertson, Hume, and Gibbon in the eighteenth century; of the great work of Macaulay in the nineteenth century. It was on the Orations of Cicero that Wyatt modelled the speech which is the earliest example in our language of oratorical eloquence; and, from that day to this, the speeches to which, if we wished to vindicate our fame in oratory, we should point, are the speeches which have followed most closely the same noble models. No names stand so high on the roll of our Parliamentary orators as the names of Bolingbroke, Pulteney, Chesterfield, the two Pitts, Burke and Fox; and no names stand higher on the roll of forensic orators than those of Somers, Mansfield, and Erskine. It is notorious that they all gloried in their familiarity with the ancient masterpieces—the masterpieces of Demosthenes and Cicero—and have all left testimonies of their obligations to them. And what has moulded our secular oratory has moulded our sacred oratory. On no part of our prose literature can we look with greater pride than on the sermons of our Classical Divines; and assuredly no part of our literature owes more to the influence of Greece and Rome. The dawn of the Renaissance found our pulpit oratory represented by a few rude and jejune homilies, scarcely rising above the level of the Sawles Warde or the Ayenbite of Inwyt; its close left us enriched with the Sermons of Hall and Donne, of Taylor and South, of Barrow and Tillotson. If this marvellous transformation is to be explained partly by the progress which secular literature had made, and partly by the influence of the writings of the Fathers, it is to be explained mainly by the influence— the direct influence—of those writers, to which the Fathers themselves were so greatly indebted. Hall and Donne, for example, are in style and diction close imitators of Seneca; and to Seneca, as the author of the Consolatio ad Marciam and the Consolatio ad Helviam, belongs, it may be added, the honour of having furnished models for the Oraisons Funèbres of the French, and for what corresponds to the Oraisons Funèbres in our own language. From Plato, Taylor learned the secret of his involved harmonies, and on Plato and Chrysostom he fashioned his diffuse and splendid eloquence. What South would

would have been apart from the influence of the ancient masters
may be easily seen by comparing the passages in which he
gives the rein to the coarse vigour of his native genius, and the
passages on which his fame rests.   The inexhaustible fertility
of Barrow's intellect is to be attributed as unmistakably to the
assimilative thoroughness with which he had studied the Greek
and Roman Classics, as the pregnant energy of his expression
bears the impress of Thucydides and Aristotle.   What style is
more purely Ciceronian than the style of Tillotson, than the
style of Sherlock, than the style of Atterbury ?

But no portion of our literature is rooted more deeply in the
literature of antiquity than our criticism.   Dryden has some-
where remarked that—

> ' One poet is another's plagiary,
> And he a third's till they all end in Homer.'

Till the end of the last century, it may be said with literal
truth that from the publication of Wilson's Art of Rhetoric,
in 1553, it would be difficult to mention a single theory on the
principles of composition, a single important critical canon,
with the exception of the doctrine of the unities of time and
place, which are not to be traced originally to the ancient critics.
It is a great mistake to suppose, as it almost always is supposed,
that we derived our principles of criticism from France.   Our
own criticism and French criticism sprang from a common
source.   It was derived directly from Aristotle and Longinus,
from Cicero, from Horace, from Quintilian, and from the
author of the Dialogus de Oratoribus, all of whom had been
studied in England long before they had been translated into
French.   We have only to open the treatises of Wilson, Elyot,
Ascham, Sidney, Webbe, Gascoigne, Puttenham, and others, in
the reign of the Tudors, and such a work as Jonson's Dis-
coveries, in the reign of James I., to see how closely the fathers
of English criticism followed in the footsteps of the ancients.
It was so with Hobbes, it was so with Cowley, it was so even
with Dryden.   That Dryden and his contemporaries read
Aristotle in a French version, and with the light of French
commentaries, is undoubtedly true.   And it is true also that
they were acquainted with contemporary French criticism.
But Aristotle in a French dress is Aristotle still, and as contemporary French criticism was itself so largely indebted to
Greece and Rome, we must not confound the influence of Rapin
and Bossu with the influence of those writings on which Rapin
and Bossu themselves drew so largely.   For one reference in
Dryden's Prefaces to a French critic, we find a dozen to an
                                                    ancient.

ancient. Longinus, indeed, owed his popularity to Boileau, but he had been translated into our language long before Boileau's version appeared, and had, as early as the first quarter of the seventeenth century, begun to affect critical opinion in England. Between the death of Dryden and the death of Johnson our critical literature passed still more completely under the yoke of the ancients. Every precept in the Essay on Criticism is drawn or deducted from the Ars Poetica, from the Institutes, or from the De Sublimitate. The Treatise on the Bathos is a parody of the Treatise on the Sublime. The literary papers of Addison, and of Addison's coadjutors, follow implicitly the same guides. The literary essays of Hume betray in every page their indebtedness to the ancient critics. Horace and Quintilian furnish Johnson with his canons and his standards. No one can read the critiques in the Lives of the Poets without being struck with their similarity to the critiques in the tenth book of the Institutes. The terse and epigrammatic judgments, at once narrowly discriminating and superficially just, which Quintilian passes on the Greek and Roman writers, are the exact counterparts, as well in spirit and matter as in expression, to Johnson's judgments on our own poets. If we pass from Johnson to Hurd, who was, of our own countrymen, incomparably the subtlest literary critic of the eighteenth century, and who, by his practice of habitually referring phenomena to principles, and of distinguishing between accidents and essence, may be regarded as the forerunner of modern philosophical criticism, we simply pass from a student of Horace and Quintilian to a student of Aristotle and Longinus. With what care, with what sympathy, to what great advantage, Hurd had studied both the Poetics and the De Sublimitate, will be apparent to any one who will compare his Notes on the Ars Poetica, the earliest of his works, with his Dissertations on the Idea of Universal Poetry, on the Provinces of the Drama, and on Poetical Imitation, discourses which by no means deserve the oblivion into which they appear to have fallen. But we must not pursue this subject further. We have said enough to show, that no account of the history of criticism in England can be other than miserably inadequate which does not trace it to its source, and that to trace it to its source is to trace it to the classics of the old world.

We contend, therefore, that the history of English Literature can never be studied properly unless it be studied in connection with the literatures of Greece and Rome, and that to study it without reference to those literatures is as absurd as it would be to study the history of ethics and metaphysics, or the

history of sculpture and architecture, without reference to the
ancient schools.   It may perhaps be urged that, as Celtic and
Teutonic elements enter so largely into the composition of the
English temper and the English genius, and that as the literatures of modern Italy, of France, and of Germany have succes-
sively affected our own, it is, from an historical point of view,
as necessary to take them into consideration as it is the older
literatures.   This is partly true, but this is not practical.   In
no school of literature could a student be expected to read, in
addition to Greek and Latin, half-a-dozen other languages, and
among those languages Celtic, Anglo-Saxon, and German.
And even if this were practicable, comparatively little would
be gained.   Neither Cædmon's Paraphrase nor the Tain Bo
would throw much light on the genesis of Paradise Lost, nor
would the Ayenbite of Inwyt throw much light on the genesis
of the Sermons of Taylor and Barrow.   The only modern
literature which has materially affected us is the Italian.   But
it is useless to discuss impossibilities.   The question simply
resolves itself into this, whether, if English Literature is to be
seriously studied, it should be studied in connection with the
literatures of the modern world, as is, we believe, now being
proposed at Oxford; or whether, on the other hand, it should
be connected with the study of the Classics.   In what way that
question should be answered we have endeavoured to point
out.

But if in tracing the development of our literature it is
necessary at every step to refer to the ancients in studying the
literature itself, in regarding it, that is to say, in its spiritual,
its ethical, its æsthetic aspects, in considering its structure and
its style, how greatly do we gain by comparing its masterpieces
with the masterpieces of Greece and Rome.   To go no further
than the tragedies of Shakspeare : what could be more interesting, what more profitable, than to compare them with the
tragedies of the Attic stage, to compare them, for example, with
the tragedies of Sophocles; to note how the same truths, the
same passions, the same sentiments, find utterance in both ; to
observe how similarly each deals with the great problem of
destiny and free-will, with the doctrine of the mean, with the
doctrine of retribution, with the relations of the State to the
individual and of the individual to the State ; to mark how
subtly in each the real and the ideal are blended ; to compare
their use of irony, to watch the same art working in obedience
to the same eternal and unchanging laws directing them in the
mechanism of their expression, and the same inspired wisdom
guiding them in their interpretation of life.   How much,
for

for instance, would a comparative study of Macbeth and the Agamemnon, of Henry V. and the Persæ reveal. What better commentary is to be found on those marvellous fictions which, in the phrase of their creator, hold the mirror up to human nature, than the writings of the subtlest analyst of human nature who has ever lived, the author of the Ethics and of the third book of the Rhetoric? Indeed, if some scholar would illustrate the dramas of Shakspeare by pertinent references to Aristotle's treatises, he would add greatly to the interest of both, for it would be seen with what exactness each of these students of human nature, though separated by nearly two thousand years, has arrived independently at the same truths, and corroborate each other. We contend then that Aristotle contributes to the elucidation of Shakspeare, as Shakspéare contributes to the elucidation of Aristotle.* That such poems as Lycidas and the Progress of Poesy have been the delight of thousands, who have never opened a Greek or Roman classic, is no doubt true, but it would be absurd to pretend that their pleasure would not have been ncreased tenfold had they been scholars; it would be absurd to pretend that the full significance, the race, so to speak, and flavour of either the one poem or the other could have been appreciated by them. A reader who knows nothing of Sophocles and Virgil may feel the charm of such a diction as the Laureate's, of such a diction as the diction of In Memoriam, or the diction of the Princess; but how much will he miss, how many of the

$$\text{ὠκέα βέλη}$$
$$\text{φωνᾶντα συνετοῖσιν}$$

must fall flat on him.

But apart from particular reasons for associating the study of English Literature with that of the Literature of Antiquity,— apart from considerations of historical development and the interpretation of this author or that author, there remains the great fact, that by the universal consent of civilized mankind the ancients have in almost every department of the Literæ Humaniores approached most nearly to perfection. Out of their very names have been coined synonyms for the excellencies which severally distinguish them. What they have wrought has become archetypal. They stand, indeed, in the same relation to polite letters as the Old Masters stand to painting. It is possible, no doubt, for a painter, whose eyes have never rested on a Dutch or an Italian masterpiece, to produce work of a very

---

* There is not, of course, the smallest reason for supposing that Shakspeare ever read a line of Aristotle, either in the original or in a translation.

high

high order, and it is certainly possible for a poet who has never
read Homer or Horace, to write poetry which Homer and Horace
would not have been ashamed to own.   But what applies to an
artist will not apply to a critic.   A man, who set up as a judge
of pictures without being familiar with the chief works of the
Great Age, or if he knew them, knew them only by copies,
might pass for a connoisseur with the crowd, but would find his
opinions little appreciated by experts.   It is the same, or should
be the same with the critic, with the student of Literature.   The
Homeric Poems, the Æneid and Georgics, the Attic Tragedies,
the Lyrics of Pindar and Horace, the best of the Platonic
Dialogues, the best Orations of Demosthenes and Cicero—these
are his Michael Angelos, his Da Vincis, his Raphaels.   These
are his standards, these are his touchstones.   We are no bigoted
admirers of the ancients.   We believe that the great tragedies of
Shakspeare are, considered merely as works of art, at least equal
to the Œdipus Rex, and that if they be estimated by the powers
of mind displayed in them they would, in sheer weight of in-
tellectual bullion, make the dramas of Æschylus, Sophocles,
Euripides, and Aristophanes, massed together, kick the beam.
No discerning judge would hesitate to say that the comedies of
Molière are incomparably superior to the comedies of Terence.
We should be quite prepared to prove categorically that Burke's
speech on the Nabob of Arcot's debts and on conciliation with
America are greater oratorical feats than the Verrines or the
Antonian Philippics.   We rank Burns with Catullus, we rank
Dryden above Juvenal.   We think Walpole and Gray wrote
better letters than the younger Pliny, and we should pronounce
the History of the Decline and Fall to be a more impressive
monument of human genius and of human skill than the History
of the Peloponnesian War.   But this does not prove, as is often
absurdly asserted, that familiarity with the works of modern
writers would, in the education of a student of literature, be an
equivalent for familiarity with the works of the ancients.
By none indeed has this been more emphatically pointed out
than by those who have themselves been the most distinguished
ornaments of our vernacular literature.   ' Let persons of limited
conception,' says Burke, in a passage which educational legislators would do well to remember, ' think what they will of
classical learning, it has ever been and ever must be the first
principle of a taste, not only in the Arts, but in life and morals.
If we have any priority over our neighbours, it is in no small
measure owing to the early care we take with respect to a classical education which cannot be supplied by the cultivation of
                                                                                    any

any other branch of learning.'* But it is useless to discuss a question about which, among competent judges, there never have been and there never can be two opinions.

On all grounds, then, on historical, on critical, on general, the necessity of associating the study of classical literature with that of our own, if our own is to be studied properly, is obvious, and it is equally obvious that if this is to be done, it can be done only with the aid of the Universities. Why Oxford and Cambridge should not deem the interpretation of our national literature as worthy of their serious attention as the study of our national history—how it has come to pass that, while the most liberal and enlightened views prevail with regard to the teaching of history, the teaching of literature is either neglected altogether, or abandoned contemptuously to dilettants and philologists—is a problem which we at least are quite unable to solve. But it points, we think, to the great defect, to the only serious defect in our University system. From the days of Pope, Oxford and Cambridge have been commonly taunted, and we fear justly, with attaching too much importance to philology, with regarding the works of great poets and of great orators, not as the expression of genius and art, but as mere material for verbal criticism, as mere monuments of language. Until lately, the literary and æsthetic value of the Greek and Roman classics has undoubtedly been too little considered, the method of interpreting them being almost exclusively the method of the technical scholar, a method which cannot be too highly appreciated when regarded as a means to an end, or too strongly condemned when regarded as an end in itself. We have, however, recently observed with pleasure that, on the subject of classical exegesis, more liberal views are beginning to prevail. We wish we could discern the same promising symptoms in the case of our own Literature, but here unhappily the dominion of philology is absolute. How obstinately indeed University legislators, or at all events an important section of them, appear to be bent on discountenancing any other than a philological interpretation of that Literature has recently received a memorable illustration. About three years ago, a party at Oxford, who were strongly in favour of an intelligent study of our national classics being encouraged in the University, and who were

---

* 'Letter to Parr.' Parr's Works, Johnstone's edit., vol. i. p. 200. 'It is with the deepest regret,' writes Scott, referring to his neglect of classical studies, ' that I recollect in my manhood the opportunities of learning which I neglected in my youth, and through every part of my literary career I have been pinched and hampered by my ignorance; it is a loss never to be repaired.'—*Autobiography.*

anxious

anxious to raise English Literature to its proper level in education, so far prevailed as to obtain the consent of Convocation to the foundation of an English Chair. A Chair of English Literature was accordingly founded and liberally endowed. A Board of Electors was appointed. As there was already a Chair of Celtic, a Chair of Anglo-Saxon, a Chair of Comparative Philology, and as therefore the philological study of English had been amply provided for, it was confidently expected that the choice of the electors would fall on the sort of teacher contemplated by the originators of the movement. But Philology triumphed. The Board discovering, that though the language of Cædmon and the language of Oisin had received the attention they deserved, the dialect of Robert of Gloucester and William of Shoreham had not, determined to seize this opportunity to remedy the defect. Availing themselves of a quibble on the word 'language'—for the Statute authorizing the foundation of the Chair happened, by a mere accident, to couple the word 'language' with 'literature'—they succeeded in ignoring the object for which the Chair was founded, and proceeded to elect, at a permanent salary of about 900*l.*, a Professor for the interpretation of Middle English. Such was the fate of a movement which might, and probably would, have formed an era of incalculable importance in education. It is indeed half-painful, half-ludicrous, to reflect that at the present moment, in Oxford alone, upwards of 3000*l.* a year are expended on the interpretation of writings which are confessedly of no literary value, and of interest only as monuments of language, while not one farthing a year is spent on the interpretation of works which are the glory of our country.

We have, however, little doubt that an anomaly so extraordinary and so disgraceful will not to be tolerated much longer. We feel confident that English Literature, in the proper sense of the term, will sooner or later receive the recognition to which at the centres of culture it is assuredly entitled. Our only fear is either that it may be considered too exclusively with reference to itself, or that it may be assigned a place in some other part of the curriculum than that part to which, as we have endeavoured to show, it properly belongs. It would, we submit, be a great mistake to make it form a portion, as some propose to do, of the curriculum of a School of Modern Literature, and to treat it only in connection with Modern Literature. It would be a still greater mistake to attach it collaterally, as others propose, to the curriculum of the Modern History School, and to consider it mainly in its relations to Modern History. To prescribe, on the other hand, an independent
pendent

pendent and uncomparative study of it, to deal with it, that is
to say, as a subject bounded by and complete in itself, would
be equally objectionable because equally insufficient. Its
proper place is the place which we have indicated—with the
literatures which are at the head of all literatures, with the
literatures which nourished it, which moulded it, which best
illustrate it.

What is needed, and we venture to add imperatively needed,
is the institution of a school which shall stand in the same
relation to pure literature, to poetry, oratory, and criticism, as
the present school of history stands to history, and as the
present school of Literæ Humaniores stands to philosophy. In
both these schools, in the former as it is about to be constituted, in the latter as it always has been constituted, the historical and philosophical classics of the old world are most
properly associated with those of the new. No hard-and-fast
line is drawn between philosophers and historians who write in
Greek or Latin, and philosophers and historians who write
in English. Both are studied not for the light which they may
happen to throw collaterally on the structure and history of
language, but for the light which they throw on the subjects
which are severally treated by them. Herodotus and Thucydides are accordingly included in the same curriculum as
Clarendon and Gibbon. The Republic and the Ethics
are read side by side with the essay on the Human Under-
standing and the Enquiry concerning the Principles of
Morals. Thus not only are the masterpieces of ancient and
modern philosophy brought home to the student, but their
relations to each other are rendered intelligible. ‘The work,’
says the Regius Professor of Modern History at Oxford, ‘which
I have come to do is to point out that the work of Kleisthenes,
of Licinius, of Simon of Montfort, are parts of one living whole,
a whole of which every stage needs to be grasped by the same
faculties, to be studied by the same methods.’ Why, we would
ask, should not the same view be taken of the work of Sophocles
and Shakspeare, of Cicero and Burke? Are they not also ‘parts
of one living whole’? Is not poetry, poetry; oratory, oratory;
criticism, criticism in whatever language they may be ex-
pressed? And is not the study of literature the study of its
development generally, and of its masterpieces particularly?
Why the works of a philosopher or a historian who writes in a
classical language should be studied as illustrating philosophy
and history, while the works of a poet or of an orator who
writes in a classical language should be regarded as mere
material for construing,—why University men should be expected

pected to know in what way modern metaphysics have been affected by Plato and modern ethics by Aristotle, and should not be expected to know in what way modern poetry has been affected by Homer and Horace, and modern oratory by Demosthenes and Cicero—we cannot understand. But of one thing we are quite sure, that it is high time, both in the interests of classical literature and of our own literature, to take this question into serious consideration, and to see whether the institution of such a school, or of some school similar to such a school as we have suggested, be indeed practicable. What the nation has a right to expect from the Universities is, that they should provide as adequately for the dissemination of literary culture as they have provided for other branches of education. And this we contend they can never do if, on the one hand, for the study of the two leading and master literatures of the world, the literatures which are and must always be the basis of the education of which we are speaking, they substitute the study of what certain educational theorists are pleased to call modern equivalents; and if, on the other hand, they continue to exclude our own literature from their curriculum.

Of the necessity of the Universities directing their attention to this important subject, no further proof is required than the contrast between the high standard of classical, historical, and scientific teaching throughout the kingdom and the deplorably low standard, all but universal, in the teaching of English literature. In many places it is degraded into mere cram-work, into prescribing so many pages of a primer or manual to be got by heart. In other places it goes no further than the purely philological study of single works. If a more enlightened exegesis is anywhere employed, it is the result of simple accident. And what is true of the standard of teaching is true of the standard of production. A work analogous to the work which stands at the head of this article would, we believe, in any other department of learning and culture, be impossible. One tithe of its blunders and absurdities would have ruined instantly a book treating of Greek or Roman poetry, or discussing some point in modern history. No one indeed can compare an average review or magazine article on a classical, a historical, or a scientific subject, with an average article dealing with a purely literary subject, without being struck with the immense superiority of the former to the latter. The first we feel to be the work of a man who has had an efficient training, who is master of his subject, who is possessed with his subject, and who is conscious that he is addressing readers who will meet him halfway. In the second, we are fortunate if we do not
find

find all the indications of half-knowledge and of gross ignorance, and of half-knowledge and gross ignorance conscious of being able to assume without detection the garb and semblance of intelligence and learning. An editor of a scientific or historical Review has not the least difficulty in finding contributors who are able to write up to the high level required in such subjects. It is notorious that editors of literary Reviews are constantly under the necessity of accepting articles, the inferiority of which they are themselves the first to admit. For the existence of this extraordinary anomaly, the Universities, and the Universities only, are responsible. We owe it to them—and it is to their honour—that the standard is so high, and those who maintain it so numerous in the one case. We owe it to them—and it is not to their credit, that the standard is so low, and those anxious to raise it so few, in the other case. And till they are prepared to take active measures, and to extend to the study of literature, and especially to the study of our vernacular litera-ture, the protection they have extended to other branches of education—so long will this state of things continue; so long will mediocrity, sciolism, and ignorance prevail; so long will our presses continue to pour forth such books as the book on which we have been animadverting, and so long will our leading literary journals continue to pronounce them 'volumes not to be glanced over and thrown aside, but to be read twice and consulted often.'

ART.

ART. II.—1. *Sport.* By W. Bromley-Davenport. London, 1886.

2. *The Badminton Library.* Edited by the Duke of Beaufort, K.G. Fishing : by H. Cholmondeley-Pennell. London, 1886.

3. *Salmon Problems.* By Willis Bund. London, 1885.

4. *Autumns on the Spey.* By A. E. Knox, M.A., F.L.S. London, 1872.

5. *Twenty-fifth Annual Report of the Inspector of Fisheries (England and Wales).*

6. *The Treatyse of Fysshynge with an Angle,* attributed to Dame Juliana Berners, reprinted from the *Book of St. Albans.* London, 1827.

IN a highly critical age it is dangerous to affirm the authorship of even well-known works, and we are not disposed to examine whether the quaint ' Treatyse of Fyshynge with an Angle,' one of the earliest if not the earliest of the many essays on the subject extant in English, was or was not by Dame Juliana Berners. It suffices us to point out the ever-growing support attaching to the contention with which the quaint little work opens. ' Which ben,' asks the author, ' the meanes and the causes that enduce a man into a merry spyryte : Truly to my beste dyscrecōn it seemeth good dysportes and honest games in whom a man Joyeth without ony repentannce after.' It would be rash to assert that there are no sports and games of their joy in which many have much repentance, but the popularity of such of our national pastimes as need no ' sermons and soda-water the day after ' is happily always on the increase.

For his or her preference of angling over other sports the writer of the treatise we have quoted advances wisely grotesque reasons :

' Huntynge is toe laboryous, for the hunter must alwaye renne and folowe his houndes : traueyllynge and swetynge full sore, and blowynge tyll his lyppes blyster.' . . . ' Hawkynge is laboryous and noyouse also as me seemyth.'

and

' Fowlynge is greuous.' But the ' angler maye haue no colde nor dysease nor angre but if he be causer hymself. For he may not lese at the moost, but a lyne or an hoke . . . and other greyffes may he not have, sauynge but yf ony fysshe breke away after that he is take on the hoke, or elles that he catche nought . . . and yet atte the leest he hath his holsom walk and mery at his ease, a swete ayre of the swete sauoure of the meede floures. . . . Thus have I prouyed

in

in myn entent that the dysporte and game of anglynge is the very meane and cause that enduceth a man in a merry spyryte.'

The writer knows nought of fishing in its present development. The angling discussed in the ' Treatise ' was the quiet and contemplative art in which Izaak Walton delighted, rather than the active and exciting pursuit which, in one at least of the most popular of Scotch country houses, has made the attractions of the forest and moor subordinate to those of the river. And it is to considerations unsuspected in the ' Treatyse ' that we are inclined to attribute the hold which salmon-fishing has upon the affections of a generation sadly apt to suffer from satiety. Two of these we may mention. Salmon-fishing will never pall, because of its uncertainty. In all other sports the possibility of forecasting the amount of success obtainable under given conditions is greater than it is in salmon-fishing; and this adds a zest which will ever be attractive so long as the sporting instincts of Englishmen are as wholesome and as reasonable as they are now. Secondly, there can be no coercion in salmon-fishing. Birds and beasts of all kinds are taken by the *force majeure* of the hunter. Their means of escape are limited to avoidance of attack. In salmon-fishing (and of course under that head we do not include practices of snatching or leistering, both of which are illegal), unless the fish performs a substantive act of his own volition—to wit, taking the bait—he is not captured. Herein is a cause which frees salmon-fishing from the assaults of the most tender-hearted and refined moralist. The salmon becomes a prey by the performance of an act of depredation.

καὶ σ' εἷλε θηρῶνθ' ἡ τύχη

the successful fisher might say to him. He is the biter bit, the ' desolator desolate, the victor overthrown.' Man is a beast of prey, and unquestionably most of his favourite pursuits have for their object the destruction of animal life. But of all such pursuits, and of all such destroying of life, the least objectionable, even from the ultra-humanitarian point of view, is the capture of salmon by angling.

Of the first of these characteristics we find a thorough appreciation in the lively and interesting volume which we have placed at the head of the works referred to in this article. The late Mr. Bromley-Davenport was a thorough sportsman in every sense of the word. He was not one of those who measured success by mere quantity. To him the value of an achievement depended much upon the difficulties to be overcome; and in the four pleasant Essays upon Fox-hunting,
Salmon-fishing,

Salmon-fishing, Covert-shooting, and Deer-stalking, included
in the volume before us, he presents a picture of English sport
in the form in which it is most likely to maintain its hold
upon our national ideas, and to exercise a useful influence upon
our national character.

'It is the unknown,' he tells us, 'which constitutes the main charm
and delight of every human creature's life. Uncertainty is the salt
of existence. . . . Whatever is reduced to a certainty ceases to
charm, and but for the element of risk or chance—uncertainty, in
short—not only every sport or amusement, but even every operation
and transaction of this world, would be tame and irksome. If we
foreknew the result we would seldom do anything, and would
eventually be reduced to the condition of the bald, toothless, toeless,
timid, sedentary, and incombative man of the future, foreshadowed
recently by a very advanced writer.'

Salmon-fishing has this charm in a very high degree, and
we are not sure that Mr. Bromley-Davenport was justified in
ranking fox-hunting above it. It is absolutely impossible to
predict what will be the result of any day's fishing. If a man
is not prepared to meet with disappointment he had better not
be a salmon-fisher. The causes which conduce to failure are in
themselves multitudinous. The river is too high or too low,
the water too thick or too clear; the weather too stormy, or the
sunshine too bright; the fish have been too long in the river,
or they are swimming up it; the wind is in the wrong quarter,
or there is thunder about. These, and many other such, are
conditions which discourage hope. But more than this. There
are few salmon-fishers who have not had their spirits raised to
the highest pinnacle by the conditions of the day, to find themselves reduced ere evening to a state of blank despondency.
The conditions may have been perfect; water, weather, and fish,
may all have been in such a state as to lead to the anticipation
of great success; and yet the end of a hard day's fishing has
found the angler with nothing whatever to show in return for
his wearied shoulder and stiff back. On the other hand, success
comes when least expected. On the Tweed, on one occasion, an
experienced fisherman was waiting for a brother angler to go
with him to a distant pool. With him was a tyro who had
never thrown a fly, and who, with some persuasion, was induced
to try a few casts. With his first he produced web-like circles
of gut on the water; his second sent the fly out fairly straight;
with his third he hooked and killed one of the largest and best
salmon seen for several seasons on the Tweed.

'Cuivis dolori remedium patientia,' must certainly be the
true angler's motto. Without patience, persistent and unfailing,

no

no one can succeed as a salmon-fisher. He must be discouraged by no failure however prolonged, crushed by no disaster however severe. How great may be an angler's trials Mr. Bromley-Davenport graphically describes, when he tells us how after a three hours' fight with 'an ideal monster of his dreams'—we may trust Mr. Bromley-Davenport, although the lost fish are ever large—he brings him within easy reach of the gaffer, who, demoralized and unnerved by the presence of the largest salmon he has ever seen, misses him, once, twice, thrice, and then

' a deadly sickness comes over me as the rod springs straight and the fly dangles useless in the air. Is it possible? Is it not a hideous nightmare? But two minutes ago blessed beyond the lot of angling man—on the topmost pinnacle of angling fame. The practical possessor of the largest salmon ever taken with a rod, and now, deeper than ever plummet sounded, in the depths of dejection.'

Those who have had less trials can well understand how his mind, already depressed, yielded 'to the influence of the hour and went to zero;' and how 'despondency—the hated spirit—descended from her foggy cloud and was his inseparable companion all the way home.' But those also who know of how sterling an Englishman Mr. Bromley-Davenport's too early death deprived his country and the world of sport, can have no difficulty in asserting, that the hated spirit had no long sway, but that ere another day had dawned hope once more sprang eternal in the human breast, and the chances of success were once more seen in a rosy light.

It is not in anglers to command success, and no amount of preparation and care make sure of the huge bags which are feasible enough in the case of pheasants, partridges, or even grouse. But remarkable feats have been performed, and we are able to give particulars of some of the most notable of these. Seven years ago three Englishmen found themselves on the banks of the grand Cascapedia river, in the Province of Quebec. They fished steadily through June and July, after the 19th of which month one of their number left. The other two remained for a fortnight more of fishing. Between them they killed 622 salmon, which together weighed 15,648 lbs., and of which 128 were of 30 lbs. and upwards. Their two best days deserve special record, as shown in the table on the next page.

The totals of the two days we have referred to, and the individual performance of Mr. Ellis on the 18th of June, will stand out pre-eminently whenever facts of angling are examined. We doubt whether a like result has ever followed fair rod-fishing. It must, however, be remembered that the river, which yielded
such

			Total.	Weight.
1879 June 16　..	Hon. C. Ellis　..　..　..	37, 28, 28, 28, 26, 26, 25, 25, 25, 24, 24, 23, 22, 22 ..　..　..	14	363
„　　..	L. Iveson　..　..　..　..	37, 26, 25, 25, 24, 24, 22, 12, 10	9	205
„　　..	Captain G. A. Percy　..	32, 32, 31, 30, 29, 29, 29, 28, 26, 25, 25, 9　..	12	325
				893
July 11　..	Hon. C. Ellis　..　..　..	34, 32, 29, 28, 25, 25, 24, 24, 24, 24, 24, 23, 22, 22, 22, 20, 13	17	415
..	L. Iveson　..　..　..　..	36, 36, 31, 29, 26, 25, 25, 25, 24, 23, 22, 11, 10	13	323
„　　..	Captain G. A. Percy　..	31, 31, 28, 25, 25, 24 ..　..　..	6	164
				927
June 18　..	Hon. C. Ellis　..　..　..	38, 36, 36, 32, 32, 32, 31, 30, 24, 24, 24, 22, 22, 21, 21, 20, 20	17	465

such extraordinary sport, had not been over-fished, and that the
skill and perseverance of the anglers had the advantage of comparatively virgin soil. The Cascapedia will probably always be
a productive river. This year the present Governor-General,
Lord Lansdowne, got four fish, averaging thirty-four pounds, in
a short evening. But it is not likely that the yield of 1879
will be equalled. At home the rivers in all parts of the United
Kingdom are, even as regards the most closely-preserved waters,
sedulously fished, and similar results can hardly be expected.
For salmon, like other animals, learn by experience. 'Salmon,'
says Sir H. Davy in his 'Salmonia,' 'appear to me to learn,
when they have been some time in the river, that the artificial
fly is not food even without being touched by the hook.' The
fish in a river, where day after day flies of all patterns are
played in all fashions, become shy, and will not rise. And
a fish on his return to a well-fished river is, we imagine, more
easily brought to a state of shyness than when the waters he
frequents are not haunted by artificial lures. Nevertheless remarkable sport has occasionally been yielded. On 'Sprouston
Dub,' on the Tweed, two rods, fishing alternate hours, killed on
October 29th, 1884, sixteen salmon and one grilse thus :—

First

First Rod. G. D. W.		Second Rod. R. D. B.	
1st hour	18 lbs. 19 „	21 lbs. 13 „	2nd hour.
3rd hour	25 „ 23 „	16 „ 20 „	4th hour.
5th hour	18 „ 20 „ 27 „	8 „ 18 „ 29 „	6th hour.
7th hour	20 „	18 „ 24 „	8th nour.

8 Fish, 170 lbs.

9 Fish, 167 lbs.

Sprouston Dub is a favourite pool. In October 1873, a single rod killed 13 salmon and 3 grilse, weighing 332 lbs.; and next month a still more successful angler got 21 fish, weighing 370 lbs.

On the lower part of the Upper Merton water, also on the Tweed, Mr. Farquhar got 18 fish on November 9th, 1885. Weights: 24, 21, 21, 20, 20, 19, 19, 18, 17, 17, 16, 16, 10, 10, 9, 8, 7, 6 lbs.

> November 10, Lord Brougham, 17 fish.
> „ 11, Mr. Farquhar, 11 fish.
> „ 12, Lord Brougham, 12 fish.
> „ 13, Mr. Farquhar, 10 fish.
> „ 14, Lord Brougham, 4 fish.

Altogether in the whole week Mr. Farquhar got 51 fish, and Lord Brougham 44.

On 28th of September, 1885, at Taymount on the Tay, the Hon. and Rev. R. Liddell killed 6 salmon and 14 grilse.

But perhaps if the condition of the fish caught is considered, as well as the sport they afford, the best rod-fishing in the United Kingdom is that in the lower portion of the Spey. The Duke of Richmond and Gordon fishes about ten miles of water above and below Gordon Castle; and here, in the months of September and October, a run of perfectly fresh fish, often of great weight, occurs every year. In the first nine days of one notable October, 210 fish were landed, the details of the best day being as follows:—

'21, 18, 18, 11, 9; 9½; 14, 15, 11; 20, 17, 14, 11; 27, 17½, 8½; 23; 29, 21, 14; 23, 10, 9, 9; 22, 18, 17, 17, 16, 15, 15, 10½, 10, 10, 9; 21, 20, 20, 16; 19½, 18, 11, 9, 8; 17, 16 lbs. Total, 46 fish. 714½ lbs.'

In 1885 the results were even better. On the 18th of September, 11 rods killed 34 fish, the heaviest weighing 27 lbs.;

ten

ten days afterwards, 11 rods killed 42 fish, the heaviest 28 lbs. ; and on October 8th in the same year, 15 rods killed 54 fish, the heaviest 31 lbs.　These results are wonderfully good, even when we bear in mind the fact that the anglers, among whom were several ladies, were both experienced and skilful.

As regards size of individual fish, it is highly probable that the largest fish of all are rarely captured by a rod.　A few years ago, however, Lord Ruthven killed on the Tay a fish of 52 lbs. In 1885, as we learn from the recent Report of the Scotch Fishery Board (4th Report, p. lxxix), the largest fish taken by the rod on the Tay was captured on the Stobhall water and weighed 47 lbs.　On the Forth the two largest captured weighed 38 lbs. and 36 lbs.　A great number of fine salmon were taken on the Aberdeenshire Dee, which yielded the largest fish of the season to the rod, weighing 57 lbs.　It was captured by the keeper on the Ardoe water.　Occasionally there appears in a newspaper an account of the capture of exceptionally large fish, but we fear that fish are sadly apt to grow ; and un-authorized statements, even if uncontradicted, must be accepted with caution.

As of other pursuits, so of fishing, the methods are many. There are those who maintain that the sole pleasure worth having consists in hooking the fish, and more than one angler has been known who habitually handed his rod to his attendant, from the feeling that the killing of the fish afforded no possible enjoyment.　On the other hand, there are some who delight in having the fish hooked for them, and who only wield the rod when there is a fish at the end of the line.　Forced to choose between the two, we should unquestionably adopt the former practice.　But there is happily no such compulsion.　Keen gratification can, we hold, be obtained from both the hooking and the playing of a salmon, and if the river abounds in dangers, it is difficult to say in which portion lies the truer pleasure. Shall we see how the matter presented itself to an experienced sportsman ?

On the 14th of October, 1868, Mr. Knox tells us, in the last chapter of his ' Autumns on the Spey,' he was fishing ' the Couperee,' one of the most extensive pools on the upper beat of the lower part of the Spey :

' I was preparing to land, but yielded to the temptation of taking one more cast before doing so, throwing again, therefore, across stream. I anxiously watched the fly as it swept round for the last time ; but just as I was on the point of drawing it out, a sudden plunge a few inches below it, followed by the apparition of a huge dorsal fin above the surface, told that I had aroused the attention of a monster, though